LULLABIES FOR

Majo Delgadillo

Lullabies for the End of the World

*bakstenen*huis
PUBLISHING

Dark Matter First published in Camas Magazine, Spring 2019
Lovestory First published in Carte-Blanche Magazine, Spring 2019

ISBN 978-90-830626-2-4
NUR 303

Bakstenen Huis Publishing B.V.
Eindhoven, the Netherlands
www.bakstenenhuis.com

Cover illustration: Valentina Jager

Content

YOUR LIFE

Here's the thing, it can happen to anyone. For example, you're home, minding your own business, hair unwashed, still wearing your pajamas with a faint smell of sweat and yesterday's dinner. And all of a sudden, you get the feeling that something's not right. And you know it might be that you have been wearing those pajamas for more than a couple of days, or that yesterday's dinner was actually the pizza from three nights before, or that the milk on your morning cereal tasted somewhat bitter but still quite alright. It could be a mix of all those things. You stop for a minute to make sure your guts are making the same usual noise. You're not nauseous, and convince yourself to take a shower and wash your hair despite the nuisance that it is. And yet, you're still feeling it. Something that's not right.

You remember that, when you were a kid, you loved puzzles, and how this one time your mother was helping you with a particularly complicated one. She figured out the pattern of the pieces and placed one of them—a little bit of blue sky—not where it belonged, but where it fitted. You'd stare at that little piece of blue sky and know that something was wrong but had no name, no vocabulary, to say that this was not the way the sky should be. Not for you. You remember the small annoyance growing sharper every time you would try and work back on that puzzle. It made no sense, that piece there. It might have been the sky for your mother, but it wasn't for you. For you, it was only wrong.

You bring your hands to the hollow part of your torso, where the ribs meet each other, right above the stomach. And there it is, exactly as it was when you were a kid: sharp, tense, unmistakable. You get in the shower again, after days and days of not doing so. You remember the time a lover said it would be amazing to take a hot shower while high. And once inside, all you could think of was how much you wanted hot chocolate so you wouldn't have to remember that, despite being your lover and not a stranger, you hated showering with strangers. Right then and there, the sharpness on your esophagus made you realize something was not right. You broke up with them soon after. You close your eyes and see fragments of your life where something like this has happened. The blue sky. The lover. But also some moments in-between. You don't scrub your body this second time. You let the hot water run down, reddening your skin as it gets hotter and hotter, and keep wondering what it might be this time around.

You recall the time you left your phone at home, trying to be a better person who can communicate with the world around them without the mediation of screens, and how it was that very same day that your father decided to have an accident. Still in the shower, you recall the taste of the breakfast you had a very hard time swallowing that morning. And, once again, the sharpness of the certainty that something was not where it should be. Something that was not wrong but certainly not right. Like the wrong piece of blue-sky fitting in a puzzle. Like putting on a sweater that shrank just barely in the dryer and wondering if it actually did shrink or if your body somehow grew larger and broader.

On that occasion—when your father had the accident—you were simultaneously ignorant and suffering for a very long time before you came back home to check your phone. When you finally called someone, maybe a sibling or your mother, they told you to rush to the hospital. And even when you knew that it was actually the time when you should start to worry, knowing that there was something wrong with a name and a cause made you happy. It lifted the weight on your chest and your guts. Contrary to your father's saying, "no news is good news," knowing made everything easier. The no news part would always make you a little bit angrier, restless. He couldn't understand the physical pain of not knowing.

You don't wash your hair every day, and lately, you have been washing it mostly out of tiny miracles: an invitation for a brunch you can't find a reason not to go to, or the sudden need to buy some more toothpaste at the supermarket. But you did wash it earlier, so now you let the hot water run through your hair, even when hot water is really bad for hair. You decide to enjoy the feeling as you wonder if you have any Advil left and if a pill can take away the heavy feeling of being burdened by things misplaced.

You start to imagine possible scenarios for whatever it is that is wrong. It shouldn't be an accident. This time you have your phone somewhere close and you think you've received zero calls. It can't be a puzzle, though it might be the way that the sky is not blue at all, not blue as you remember it to be on the image of the puzzle you never finished because, after you realized the mistake, you couldn't bear to look at it.

When you step out of the shower, you take a look at your room: clothes unwashed—as you were until a few hours ago—replacing the wallpaper and carpet, and small pieces of paper that should be trash but are still somehow part of your decoration. You try to take a deep breath, but there is that annoying imaginary obstruction on your throat. Still, you imagine the air going in and out of your body, the way you learned how to breathe when you read that book on meditation. Not that you ever did learn how to meditate. It was hard to understand how it was that you were supposed to, at the same time, picture the air going into your body—filling all the nooks of it with oxygen—and trying to maintain a blank space within your mind. This time, you picture the air going in and having to take a detour around whatever not right thing it is that has decided to camp on your body. You have to clean your room.

Maybe—you think—this feeling is less about something wrong on the outside and more about feeling good on the inside. You suddenly feel a deep sense of pride in your understanding of complex truths and disregard the fact that the inside you are thinking about is not exactly your soul but your bedroom. With your hair still wet, you start picking up clothes. It's not that you're lazy, you think. It's just that sometimes you need a signal to change bad habits. You start humming a song. Maybe it's a song that was once your favorite. Maybe you hum it as you clean because you're reminded by the heat on your skin, and the clothes on the floor, and the wetness of your hair, of the time when you knew a girl, who knew a girl, who tried to kill herself and told you all about it at a party you didn't want to go to in the first place. You knew that something was not right as soon as you got up that morning. You didn't kiss the girl because you wanted, but because she asked—after she had been crying for a while—if you were going to. She actually demanded if you were disgusted by her and her suffering, staring at you and challenging the fact that you were understanding and empathetic. That had its consequences. The heaviness on your body not disappearing after the kiss, as you had assumed would happen, but until a couple of days later when you started feeling a strange tingle on your upper lip. You wonder if it could be a cold sore this time. A cold sore once again. You know, however, how to recognize them after the first one: cold sweats, feverish dreams, and a painful, gross eruption where you once had lips. And you have never felt that specific tense sharpness on your body again before a cold sore. You recognize other things—the strange tingle, the dryness. But this notion of wrongness has nothing to do with it.

You start picking up clothes. The dress you wore a few days ago for the dinner that your ex-coworkers organized as a farewell, despite the fact that you're not going anywhere. Or maybe that's the feeling you're recognizing. Fear. The nervousness of moving. Your arms are full of clothes you wore at some point during the last month. You decide to put on something clean and look for the last thing you have left. The dress was a gift. It was probably your mother who found it on the clearance rack. It's blue. Light blue. Sky blue. You feel almost dizzy, like the feeling you usually get before you go on a rollercoaster, or after a night of drinking. Not full-on nausea, but the reflection of it. You feel drops of sweat falling from your underarms and wonder how is it possible that humans do this—discard water and salt and minerals like it's nothing. You sit for a minute. The first time you ever felt drunk, you were on a date. It was three of you: the date, your best friend, and you. You decided not to eat, recalling what the pretty girl had said on that silly TV show that you respected almost like a bible. You also didn't eat for three days so you could be lovely. And you were. But you were also just barely starting to drink, and you had beer after beer. You were lovely and lightheaded, and the drummer playing at the musty bar seemed far more beautiful than any other human you had ever seen, so you went with him after puking in the toilets, repeating to yourself that it was all A-Okay. Your room, at this moment, looks more like that bar than your actual room. Sitting on the bed, catching some air, you stare at your hands: the dryness of them, the long and dirty fingernails. You used to be so tidy. You can't even blame this on the sinking feeling on the pit of your stomach because this has been going on for a minute. A week. Maybe even a month or so. The first night you were ever drunk, your date ended up going home with your best friend. Maybe there was some sort of three-way kissing on the way. They left you home after you puked again on the curve. Once at home, you puked again on the toilet. And again the next morning. You feel like the dizziness is getting stronger, harder. You can't breathe. You feel like you're going to puke again, this day, as if there was a way of connecting yourself to all your pasts through gastric juice and only slightly spoiled milk.

What is it? You ask yourself again. What is it? This time you mouth the words. You try to speak, but after not speaking for days, your voice is a coarse and thick paste sitting at the back of your throat. The movers are coming in two days. You don't have a job anymore. At least not in this city. This could be it. You say out loud what you had been saying to everyone as if that would change anything: you're ready for an adventure. You wonder if this could be one of those instances in which that song makes sense: wouldn't it be actually ironic if what you are feeling is the sum of all the past times in which this feeling has meant something? Like, what if once in the sky—as blue as a piece of an artificial version of itself—the plane caught fire, or there was turbulence, or you had a cardiovascular accident on your way to the bathroom without ever asking for more peanuts or lime for your sparkling water? What if your father and mother forgot about you after an acute fever caused by a cold sore you gave them when you kiss them euphorically as the great ending to the sad story of your returning home? Could it be possible that the drummer from that night is dead? Could it be possible that he left you something in his will as a tribute to the night of alcohol and kissing that changed his life? Could it be that your room has not been cleaned, and you had not gotten out of bed for days on end, not because you are scared, sad, depressed, or anxious, but only as your fair side of the same tribute? You can't call the drummer. You can't call your mother, or your father, or any friend.

Part of it is that your voice is still finding its way back to this slice of reality outside your throat, but also you just realized you have no idea where your phone is. You suddenly remember, however, that you set it in silent mode before going to bed last night, or the night before. Your hair is dry. Your mouth is also dry. You'll get a glass of water as soon as you clean your room. The heaviness of your arms is directly proportional to the heaviness of your chest. You wonder if this is what being dead or nearly dead feels like: something out of place no matter how much you clean and scrub and fold. You are not going to vacuum. If this is dying, you might as well die with a dusty carpet. You can see the carpet for the first time in a while. Weirdly still grey, as if nothing had happened to it. You are not going to wash your clothes. Not today. But dirty clothes, all of them, are ready in a hamper for when you do. Maybe tomorrow. Maybe you will travel with dirty clothes and blame them for this feeling. Maybe you'll live your whole life with this feeling. Maybe you won't wash these clothes ever again.

You make the bed but don't wash the sheets. You want to go back to sleep, back to the certain numbness of dreaming. Your phone lights up from under a pillow. It doesn't make a sound. You have no strength left to read any of the messages that have one or two days waiting for you to bring them to existence, but you look anyway. It's a text from the bank—an alarm. You log into the app short of breath. As the website validates that you still are who you think you are, a sense of euphoria washes over you. Something opposite to nostalgia: a homecoming. Something pleasurable, on the verge of crying. When you finally go in, after infinite seconds, you see it. Your chest lightens. For an instant, you feel suspended in a different dimension. It has always been like this, the revelation—a moment of suspension above all earthly fears and delights.

It's staring at you, your answer, your mother's blue sky, your father's broken body, yourself too-large inside a sweater, your ex-lover, your tattered lips, your fear of flying, your ex-drummer, your first alcohol-fueled night of saliva and desire. Blinking away on the screen, all the things misplaced, joining the new one as a coven. Someone cloned your card. Someone bought a car on your name. It wasn't you, but it was almost you. You breathe. As you turn the phone down, you feel light, elated, golden. So much so that you decide to wash your clothes.

DARK MATTER

For Zachary Bushnell

For a long time, Zachary didn't really think about the sound. Every month, he said, he would imagine a different set of logical reasons for it: the neighbors, the pipes, mice, the old wooden floors, his own bones cracking, an echo of his movements saved and replayed inside the architectural carcass of the building. It was simple enough to ignore because that's how it is with old buildings—they have their own orchestras. Not like the soft humming of the AC that new homes have, but more like a crappy love song being played in the background. Something annoying only at first that, afterward, becomes comforting and charming.

I was homeless that summer. It's the summer of transitions, Zachary declared as he gave me the key to his one-bedroom apartment. We made a good team because I was living out of a suitcase and he was sleeping on a mattress on the floor. The sum of all our earthly possessions turned out to be barely a positive number. Inside the apartment I found his universe: all over the walls were diagrams and maps understandable only to him. Small pieces of paper hung like portraits, scrabbled with a language that was his, and his only. I made a contribution and hung the one photograph that I had: the one of unknown children hugging. The summer of transitions is the perfect time to start writing that novel, he said, when he caught me staring at the universe hanging from his walls. Sipping coffee, he showed me how he would make it all connect, work, speak on its own voice and on its own terms. It was not a simple task, the one on his shoulders, but he would honor it, he promised. More than writing, he was trying to figure out a way to compose a story that involved a process of randomness through a mathematical divination algorithm. Thumbtacks held together a strand of bright pink yarn that marked the points in which that process was providing the plot, post-it notes telling the story of people who were like us, napkins he would collect from coffee shops on the silent hours of early morning and, as weeks passed, letters of rejection and bills that we started collecting became a part of what he was building, too. It was a wink to reality, he said—a way to keep attachment to materiality and economy.

I could freely roam around the old neighborhood, but because the heat of summer in the city kept me inside during the day, I started hearing it too. The sound. At first, I thought it was coming from outside. It had to come from outside. Why else would it be happening at the times it was? I came home one early morning, high on coffee and sugar after spending the night at my favorite diner, and I found Zachary sitting cross-legged in the middle of the room, all limbs and knots. The lights were turned off, a painful silence pierced the apartment. He said he was really listening for the first time. He sang three adjectives, deep, dry, and patterned, in that low voice he reserved for mantras. Finally, he handed me a notebook with his notes on this subject, a beautiful scaled map of the space. He had marked the paths the sound had followed through the night, while I had been gone, in different colors.

That morning, without talking about it, we made a pact to untangle the source of the sound. The first couple of weeks were pure pleasure. We surely knew how to play detective as we both had read Bolaño. We would stay inside, drinking coffee and tea, and eating his food out. We would stare at each other suspiciously and walk around the one-bedroom apartment, recreating the paths—one or two steps into the hallway, three more until we were stepping on his mattress. Music was not allowed unless it was played through headphones, and so was laughing out loud, a rule at which we failed miserably.

We were determined to decipher what the sound was not. Old buildings have their own orchestras, after all. Sometimes it was easy: bones cracking don't really produce that kind of dry sound. He could scratch that one off. Others were harder. Luckily the neighbors moved out, with their five kids and all, and the house was inspected thoroughly for vermin. Then he had no other choice but to take those out of the list too. This is one of the first signs of possession, I told him, my knowledge coming—as always—from fiction. Echo? He asked. No, steps following you around, I replied, smiling hopefully. But we knew it wasn't possession. It couldn't be. Both our souls had decreased value in the market for such things, as there was no demand, and we were both too old to be innocent.

We didn't have a sleeping pattern during our summer with the sound, particularly because stomping and stepping became different and more nuanced once we figured out its favorite times and spots. It would be loud in early mornings, but not the loudest. It seemed mostly agile and fast, almost fragile.

When I was a toddler, I told Zach in the dark, I would wake up this early and run to my parents' bedroom on the weekends, then I would whisper really fast on my I-want-to be-taken-seriously way of speaking *canIpleaseturntheTVontowatchcartoonsataverylowvolume?* I was trying not to wake them up. He laughed quietly. After a while, when it seemed to run away, he whispered that it indeed sounded like a toddler stomp. In silence, I wished we could hear a TV turning on. A TV turning on to watch 90s cartoons at a very low volume.

I feel evangelical about the electrical universe, Zachary said one afternoon, popping his head inside the apartment while half of his body remained outside, smoking a cigarette. I was still trying to grasp the idea of a vacuum after watching videos of how things, both heavy and light things, fall inside vacuums. How can a room be turned into a vacuum? Can sound travel through a vacuum? How could that be possible if there is no air for the sound waves to travel? Is it only possible within an electrical universe? He came inside really fast and typed into his computer the name of a scientist I immediately forgot. We spent the next few hours watching recorded lectures about the electrical universe until it made sense in our minds, even though we were both humanities students, probably possessed, broke, and—at least from my side—homeless, who knew very little about astrophysics.

So, I asked, staring at the blackened screen, you don't think there is such a thing as dark matter? Well, he answered, looking at me, it can't be if the universe is electrical. But it was hard for me to believe that there could not be a thing such as dark matter. There had to. What else in the world could produce black holes, and what else in the world could stomp as decisively as the noise on the top floor of the building?

You know? He said one night while we were in the living room, tracing what sounded like soft steps upwards. I was grounded as a teenager once. Like, really grounded. I couldn't leave my room, and my parents even called my best friend's younger brother to keep an eye on me. At that point, we probably hadn't slept in more than twenty-four hours, feeding on fresh coffee and the stale bread on his pantry, listening to ourselves breathe, and to our sound guarding us like an angel or a prison guard. And then what happened? I whispered, laying on my back to stretch my muscles. I had another best friend at the time, Zachary said. He picked my girlfriend up and drove her to my house. She climbed up the window, and we spent the night together. And then, he continued, my friend picked her back up very early in the morning. So nobody knew, we both said at the same time.

I never owned a vacuum, so even the thought of the appliance was new and foreign to me. Maybe that's why, when I went back to sleep for a few hours each day, I started having nightmares of floating or falling in a space that looked exactly like the vacuums from the videos, like the chamber of the vacuum Zachary kept in a corner at all times. I think I was the most scared by the fact that there was no sound in the dream. It felt almost as cliché as being inside a bubble. Maybe that's what being deaf means.

Once a guy asked me if I would rather go blind or deaf, I told Zachary the morning after the first nightmare. And I said I would rather go blind because I could not stand to not be able to listen to music. He was busy redoing the algorithm and tracing the ways his story would go, and how the stomping affected us, as the characters we were in that universe. He went through the notes and the many maps we had gathered about our experience, to see if there was a way of transforming them into the code he was developing. It was the summer of creating this world, after all.

I poured myself some more tea and googled "is there sound in a black hole?" Apparently, there is a way of listening in a black hole, or that's what my frantic reading made me believe. I wanted to tell Zachary that even though I, too, felt evangelical about electricity, I was more and more convinced that we were co-sleeping with dark matter. With the sounds inside a black hole, and the echoes of something that was outweighing us.

We both woke up when we heard it. In one motion I slithered out of the mattress and moved as fast and quietly as possible to the living room where Zach was. The sound seemed to have multiplied. As if several sets of sounds were pounding the floor at the same time. It started really loud but, with time, it seemed to align and make sense. It was Zach who noticed it at first, not me. I was too busy and too marveled to understand its logic, but since he had been working out the logic of something else, it made sense to him.

They're dancing, he whispered. It is dancing.

And even without any perceivable music, it was true. They were. It was. Our dark matter was dancing. We had had our own dance parties in the past, both together and apart. Equally high on adrenaline and rejoicing on the momentum. I had told Zachary about how, in high school, my best friend and I had danced to Le Tigre the day before she killed herself. About being older and going out to conquer the dance floor only for the fun of it, holding someone's hand. About how a lover fell in love with me just because I loved dancing. About how, when I'm the saddest, I play music and sweat it out. About how all these things align and construct me. Then, a few months ago, we had our own dance party marking what I believed was the real beginning of our friendship, jumping up and down the living room where we were now sitting quietly. We had slept together on that very same floor. It was a vivid memory because the neighbors—the ones who moved out—used that dance party as an excuse for their own very loud gatherings ever since.

Do you remember how long we were dancing? I asked him. It should stop in an hour or so, he replied, making some room for me to lay down as we did that first night of our friendship, when I still had a home to get to, when the noise was not trying to plagiarize us.

So apparently, I announced a few days later, pulling out my phone to read from a website called *space.com*, scientists calculate the mass of large objects in space by studying their motion. Which is how they know there is dark matter, which means that even if they can't see it, they can measure the movement. And even though I had not explained why I was researching this, Zachary understood what I meant and nodded.

Dark matter? He asked, carefully, pondering, as if not completely sure if what he was saying was allowed. But why would it even want to move here, to this neighborhood? Well, I said. It's one bus away from downtown and a fifteen-minute bike ride from all the cool bars. We stared at each other's faces for a second. Then, the spell broke, and we laughed until our stomachs hurt so bad, Zachary had to write it down for his novel.

We went through the special questions people ask each other when they become friends, but instead of trying to figure each other out we were studying the motions, calculating. I had gotten a zero on the arithmetics portion of my GRE, but

Zach was very good at math, or so it seemed, and we started to pour all the information that we had, composing new and revolutionary formulas to understand dark matter. Zach wanted to add something about electricity. And what, if not electricity, are we? he asked while calculating.

I recalled how much I loved the concept of an electric heart. Of how heart failure is just a powerless heart. I hate getting shocks, I told him. I remember going up the plastic ladders at McDonald's with my socks on, and how the static made the ride as painful as it made it fun, but I stopped because I hated the shocks. I mostly hated the sound, the very loud pop that electricity creates. But that's not useful, he answered, calculator in hand. No, I know, I responded quietly, still trying to figure out what had happened the day before when the sound was much more similar to slamming doors than steps. Did your parents fight? I wondered. Slamming doors and all, he smirked. How many doors? I pursued, because in the apartment where the door slamming happened for me, we only had two possible slams, and, according to the notes, last night it seemed to have been at least four different ones.

I was going back home after the summer, but Dark Matter started to pack up earlier, so I followed. It had been so accurate before that we couldn't afford to let it down. We choreographed the scene together, Zachary, Dark Matter, and me, carefully, around the living room in which the pink strand had combined in so many places it seemed like a scene from a movie in which teenage girls make pentagrams out of macramé.

That seems like a very complicated story, I told Zachary while arranging the shoes in the order that seemed to imitate the deeps and highs of the sounds upstairs. I don't think it's just a story anymore, he answered, catching me off-guard in the midst of pushing books away from smallest to loudest. I stared at the living room in which we had danced, overslept, and underslept, eating pie and having coffee at four in the morning. I looked back at our summer of transitions and reimagined the night where our chasing of the stomping started. Him, sitting cross-legged in the middle of the living room in absolute darkness and silence. How laughter was inevitable. How the sound had decided to copy the moments of our togetherness in which we were the happiest, and the moments of our aparts where we were sad or lonely or angry or lost. I imagined how it would be when I left, after the summer, when we would never again be roommates, never again play detective, never again spend hours listening to things we couldn't grasp.

I don't know if it happened first upstairs or if it was my body, but almost immediately, for once, the sound and our apartment collided in one motion. I let my body fall unto the floor, and its weight was mimicked by our dark matter mascot. I knew that we were both there in his story, me and our beloved sound, so I said the first thing that, after that intense flashback, came to mind.

Do you remember that scientists calculate the mass of large objects in space by studying their motion? A-ha, he said, staring at me. So, if this is not a story, I said, pointing at the notes and maps, at the strand and the drawings and the formulas and calculations that had occupied our summer, if it is not a story, then it is motion, you know? I started laughing uncontrollably. If this is not a story, you are creating a movement. A large object in space that moves. Like dark matter.

And I finally got it, how vacuums work. I laid down on the floor, laughing still, trying to be quiet and see if we could still reach our neighbor. But after that, our ears just started buzzing.

THE BIRD

It will start with the eyes. With its black beak, the bird will pull out pieces of tissue. When in school, you learned how to name the gelatinous and sticky elements of eyeballs by dissecting a cow's eye. You still remember, so you repeat the process: cornea, iris, lens, aqueous humor. Hopefully, the bird will pull the whole eyeball out, stick it into the fence out in the backyard, and feast on the vitreous chamber. Otherwise, it will take longer. The bird will take small little pieces of flesh with it, coming and going until it's satiated. Then it's time to put the rest away.

"It was Leonardo Da Vinci who, interested in the mechanics of vision, invented a way to dissect a frog's eye without spilling its contents," your father would say, reading the encyclopedia he placed on the highest shelf of the only bookcase you had. The last time you opened his eyelids, around forty minutes ago, you still found a trace of the intense black behind the milky film of his eyes. An indicator of freshness.

You know how to do it, how to set the feeder for the bird. You've done it since you were ten. Put the body out through the backdoor, it will resist as bodies do, but the bird will fight and pull and fight again until it finally releases the flesh. It feels strange to study his stiffness and paleness, so different from the gleaming skin he had as a boy, running naked through the swamp that was your backyard. As a child, he would throw rocks at the bird and whisper horror stories in your ear. You would cry holding his hand, and wonder if it was true that the bird had eaten half of your baby sister's face. Your mother would come out of the house screaming, not because you were crying, but because he had scared the bird away.

"Da Vinci's technique," your father would continue before bedtime, "was to first boil the eyes in egg whites and then cut. He was the first to compare the eye with a *camera obscura.*" You can already picture it: the oval shape of his eyeball—optic nerve and all—impaled at the top of the chain-link fence you used to love climbing.

Your mother had wanted four boys, but she got twins, a boy and a girl, and a stillborn daughter. Children like you, she said constantly, were cursed. Two of the same. She was scared because you were the majority, and she didn't know what to do with the mirrored image she had for children. While she cooked or cleaned, he would give you a look—your brother—and you knew you had to run as fast as possible to get away from her. As she came near, he would give you another look, and you would just sit on the floor, waiting for your mother to catch up. When in school, it had been you and not him who was courageous enough to stomach dissecting the cow's eye. You held your breath as you cut it, pretending not to enjoy what you were doing.

If it doesn't start with the eyes, the bird will go for a chunk of his mouth. Mouths like his, like yours, are all excess. For a moment, you're almost glad that the one on your face will become a unique thing. The bird will rip a piece of his lips and take it to his palace on top of your fence. "Leonardo," your father read, "described that light rays were refracted and reflected in the eye, but its imperfect anatomy prevented the development of physiological optics."

The first time you saw a corpse, you were five. It was your baby sister. She was nameless and almost green. Her skin—because you touched her—was cardboardy and stone cold. It was difficult to believe she had been, in any way, related to you. Flesh of your flesh. At first, when the bird came, your mother seemed ready. Meat was always saved for the bird. She kept cases of frozen rabbit or deer, and she placed them outside in the backyard. But when your sister died, she started preparing stews for you. You remember the taste of the meat, the heat on your fingers while ripping it apart. "I understand now," your mother said the day of your seventh birthday, cutting both your cake and the sentence right there. You've stood here waiting for the bird for ten years.

This is the first time you'll do it without your brother. During childhood, when the bird arrived, it meant that it was time to be held at home, safely. The girls who lived further down the road, closer to town, would bring umbrellas to hit it if it ever came close. But he—your brother— and you, would go out naked and play, confident that the bird would never hurt you. How would it? Such a tiny delicate thing. Such a beautiful creature. "Look at you now," you whisper, bringing your hand close to his chest and feeling the tightness of his muscles combined with rigor mortis.

You did not fight when it was the time for your mother. He gave you a look, and you ran together until you had her pinned down. Your mother, poor thing, whose only boy was the last thing she ever saw. Your father made it much easier—hunting rifle to the head. The bird feasted on the small pieces of fat that were inside his skull. Then, you found a car wreck. Beginner's luck. It wasn't until now, seven years after becoming orphans, that you had a fight.

The long entry on the encyclopedia about Da Vinci, ended with the statement that the Italian Renaissance artist learned anatomy as a way to improve his drawings of the human form, but he also brought a scientist's eye to the discipline. You memorized that bit, and still now, you replay it with the voice of your father. You two also had to bring a scientist's eye to your discipline. You know now, for example, that his body will last for three years of the bird coming. And then, afterward, you'll figure something out.

ALGORITHMS AND ARCHITECTURE

The Bar

Nobody really likes Tinder, you know? But for some reason, we are all there: lurking and choosing and swiping left and right. It appeals to our inner dictators or something like that. Maybe.

Bear with me. I'm just making assumptions.

The thing is that I deeply hate it, but it's also fun—being a tiny god that decides the fate of others. I've been thinking about it. Now, you know, in the future. What could've happened if I had not been playing dictator? Who would it be? Would you make her laugh as much? Would she have an accent?

Love then feels very boring. It's more a matter of algorithms if you get me. A matter of architecture.

It all felt very typical. We start talking, and I don't really like you. White boy. Business school. Monolingual. The sum of the things I don't care about. But you know what they say, generally speaking, everything is more than the sum of its parts. I keep talking to you. I say, "yesokayyesyeahIknow." The whole dancing around being uninterested but not saying no. At least not yet. You keep trying. Or maybe you're not really trying, but there it is. A one-sided conversation where the girl is not really interested until you say, "Hey, you wanna get a beer?" And I'm in my pajamas at home but think, "okay, why not?" Because I'm trying to leave the house more often and know the city and understand it. Also because of the heartbreak, but we won't really talk about that.

I change and wear a black dress, makeup, and my favorite lipstick, which will be lost forever after that night and you will say you stole, but not that night, not soon thereafter either. Not until what feels like months afterward, when I need it again.

You arrive twenty minutes late, just when I'm about to leave because waiting on the street outside a bar in platform shoes and a black dress starts to feel very humiliating. You're always late, or at least that's what you claim. You made me wait, so I still don't like you. I prepare for the night to be terrible and filled with boring stories of business and school.

But it isn't.

The Corner

I don't want you to know where I live. I don't want you to come. I don't want you to see the space so small, so soon, so mine. I say goodbye on the corner I see, and use, and inhabit every day. I'm scared and slightly drunk, and you're probably drunker because you process alcohol faster than me, but that's something I'll discover later. After the apartment. After *The Evil Dead*.

I say "goodbyegoodnightnicetomeetyou," and you hug me and go in for the kiss. Maybe. Maybe it was the other way around. I'm not sure. What happens is awkward as fuck and awful, and I say, "let's try this again," because, in this world, we never get second chances. Also because I firmly believe that a kiss shouldn't be denied to anybody and that a first kiss should be nice and cute and what if I never see you again after this?

We take the chances we get, even if they are the second ones, even when those make us the first losers.

We start over. In that corner, in the breeze that is not cold but chilly (and I know this for sure because I love that word). And we kiss. And it is sweet, and it is cute, and I guess one could say I had fun.

The Studio

I throw it all away. The clothes, the papers, the pens, the trash, the memories of his presence. I mean, almost. I donate his clothes and look to see if there's anything important. I'm not a complete asshole.

I keep the PJ Harvey poster and place it over my bed, hoping he misses it. It doesn't remind me of him after the first few times. I rearrange everything, placing the new keepsakes from my friends on a shrine around my bed. A halo of protection to never feel lonely.

I buy myself some new fresh flowers every week. A healing ritual, if there ever was one.

There are still weird, weakening moments. Like when I wash the sheets over and over during the course of the first few weeks until I decide I don't want them to wear out. I just want to wear him out of them. Or, maybe, I want to wear him out of me. So I stop. They're fine. They smell like Suavitel because I hate Downy. They're crisp and soft and smell of me. I can recognize that anywhere now, what I smell like. I don't need him or you or anybody to define it anymore. It makes me happy.

That's another ritual, I guess. My own process of casting the ghosts away. Of my small room. Of the room of my own.

To reconquer.

He left the turntable that I gave him for his birthday. I see it lying there, over the table that used to be his nightstand and now is something mine with no name, job, or place. It's okay, though. I'll take it as rent. I'll take anything I can as a payback.

But after cleaning, I realize he did take Bowie's vinyls.

The motherfucker.

The Apartment

I want to write you a love poem. I know it when I'm taking off my shoes and decide to also take my socks off to feel the carpet at your place. I don't say it. Instead, I tell you that I've never had an apartment with a carpet despite moving so much when I was little but, days later, remember that I lied, because I did have a carpet in my room once. Instead, I tell you about the time I wanted to write a love poem but wrote one about cannibalism instead. I don't mind because I know you can't read it.

I make fun of your inability to understand: the language; the poem about cannibalism; me. I know there will always be this emptiness, this space between us. I command you to learn Spanish. You laugh with me. Or maybe at me. Anyway, the point is that you laugh, so I trust you.

I think you think you're charming, so you hide. Maybe you know you're charming, and that's exactly why you hide. I don't know. I don't ask. But, eventually, you tell me. Let's categorize trauma: a dead father, a mother you don't talk to. All very manageable.

You say you miss the idea of a mother, and I instantly recognize what you mean. Language, man, I tell you, it makes no sense. We put value into these things, these words, and make meanings out of them. I don't say that, either. But I tell you about my own mother. About my father. About how he never called me to go and fly kites with him. About how he rarely calls at all. You say maybe I could go with your father. We laugh.

I think this is our first shared secret.

I tell you I *make arts*, and it becomes an inside joke, and sometimes I laugh, and sometimes I feel the impostor syndrome because I'm not quite sure what that even means anymore.

You say, "I really like you, so I hope you're not conning me." I say that I just want your money, and we both laugh because out of us two, I'm not the one with student loans.

When my sister asks, I say, "he's white." When my sister calls I'm sitting on your couch and you leave the living room. When my sister starts crying on the phone, you google "the best comedies on Mexican Netflix." When you ask, I say I told her you're white.

We compare the ways in which the sun inhabits the shades in our arms and necks and torsos. There's too much sun in California. Too much torso. Too much race.

You keep the blinds closed, so you turn on the lights in the kitchen to make coffee at 8 AM, on a Sunday, before we watch a terrible movie and laugh about it for the next hour. You say, "this is your cup," so I ask you to put my name on it in glitter. You own no glitter. I promise I will get you some.

My shower's broken, so I've been showering at your place, and your towel smells terrible.

You don't know why. You promise you washed it. I keep saying I will bring my own towel, and then I do. And a toothbrush. And some bobby pins and a hair tie. An inventory of falling into the trap of love. Maybe. Maybe not really.

Maybe something closer to algorithms and architecture.

When I finally get back home, hair dripping, you say you will be busy, and I say, "okay." I say, "that's fine." I say, "alrighty, then." Thinking that was it. Thinking it was beautiful. But you say, "I'll see you next weekend," and I wish you good luck, close the car door, and walk away.

THIS STORY IS EVERYTHING

For Valentina Calvache

It's funny that you ask because I don't really recall it either. Not the particular moment when it happened the very first time and, to be honest, I only remember the last few times clearly. Maybe the last five. It might have been around the time we read that book. I mean, I read the book, but it was yours. The one that goes on about not being a linear novel, where one character who is dead becomes a second first-person narrator and watches the other narrator ride the subway in New York. That book. I think it might have started before, but that is the moment when I started to think about it, which made it real, or realer, or something.

Which is why, at first, I thought it was because of the book—a reaction of sorts. I thought I was just trying to find the relationships between fiction and my own life. That happens, right? But then it became so apparent. And, I mean, to be quite honest, now that I finally came to somehow understand how it works, I don't think I could have chosen a better person to die with so many times. A person to witness myself with. All those links and all that humanity tied together and contained in the one we have between us. Not that it was our choice, anyway, but I wanted to let you know that I do appreciate being stuck with you for the rest of my lives.

So, to answer your question, the first time I noticed, which was probably long after it had been going on, was at that 24-hour diner. It could've escaped, and I am almost sure I only noticed because I was already looking for it, because of the book and all. You got a milkshake, I got coffee, and we shared some fries. We had only known each other for a few months by then, but we were already sharing everything: food, books, clothes, beds, holidays, secrets, and as we would soon learn, deaths. It must have been about two or three in the morning. You have always hated my weird sleeping schedule, how I turn off all the lights to let you sleep, but

I'm still constantly typing on my computer, long nails clattering all through the night. But this time I'm pretty sure we were walking out of a party that was hosted by a radio station that stopped existing ten years ago. We were sitting there laughing even though your knee was fucked, my voice was gone, and we were both slightly drunk. Maybe we were laughing about that pathetic state. How being so young, we were already so sick. In any case, that was the scenario where I saw them. Us, I mean. I saw us. Except it wasn't really us, it was the waitresses.

"Do you want anything to munch on?" Said the one at the counter.

"Sure," said the one who was cleaning the tables behind me.

"Do you want a salad? I can make it for you."

"Aw. You're so sweet."

"It's because I love you!" replied the one behind me with a voice that pretended a kind of sweetness we see in television or low budget romcoms, ending the conversation with a giggle.

It could've gone unnoticed, but I knew. And you knew, right there, too. They looked nothing like us. I recall one with huge hoop earrings and the other one with long curly hair. They were taller and younger, but it wasn't that. I guess now it's pretty clear that it's not about doppelgängers. It was their relationship. It was just the tone of her voice when one of them said *I love you*. The playfulness of it all. The intimacy. The way they moved around each other and towards each other, navigating through the metallic stools and the smell of cheeseburgers. I looked at you, and you were staring. Your mouth slightly agape, and your hand still on the straw out of which you hadn't taken your sip. You knew it too.

That was the first time I noticed we had died.

It occurred to me later, it took time, but it happened, how other people would never get how this was working. Our many deaths. I think the book actually talks about that but never goes into detail about them. It just states how one sometimes dies in the subway, sometimes while leaving a party, or sometimes while forgetting the keys. And it is so simple but so hard to explain at the same time, isn't it? Because when we see ourselves as we did at the diner, we just know. We know so surely. I'm almost certain that this happens to everybody, and we are all just a reverberation of someone else's deaths. One just has to pay attention to feel it. It could be described almost as electrical currents—sonic pulses. You just know. So I can't really explain it, how does it feel, but if I had to try, it goes something like this: you listen to something—a conversation, a word between strangers. Or you see something—an eyebrow raising, you hear a shoulder cracking. You turn your head because you feel like a part of that, and then you're just a little dizzy, and that's it. You just died. Again. That simple. That clean.

The next few times were a lot more fun than the first one, or at least I remember them like that. We had grown accustomed to looking for them. We would hold hands in the cold of that winter, and I would try to make you laugh. We ate so much food we would sometimes feel sick. We kept looking. We found the bartenders who poured us free whiskey that night you ended up stealing a whole bottle. They were fun and never realized we were one and the same, a sort of future and past colliding at the same time and space. We also had the daughters of our friends, those two small sisters with the tiniest hands, the free will and stubbornness with which they rejected our kisses, and how that felt so close to us that it made us love them—and each other—more. We had the guys we would date and find each other on, and the nicknames we would mix up because we were always with each other, always looking for each other.

People noticed. They would start to joke about how we were the same person, and the funny thing is that it made us laugh to know that we were, in a sense, bound to each other forever. One constant death between us. The repetition. One constant death. Maybe that's why my favorite us has always been Genaro because I'm sure he also knew he was us, and that's why we talked for such a long time. It was refreshing for once to see someone who could tell what was going on. Someone else who had it figured out. Maybe he had read the book too. How could we know?

See, we came to understand that we could've been just one other. I never got around to actually studying dimensions and time and metaphysics as I said I would, so I only know what I can sense, and I sense that, with time, we actually combined. I'm sure Genaro was a sort of future. Many, many deaths away, maybe all the deaths we had gone through by the time we met him. He was short and skinny and brown and had a tattoo that read *heart* on his right arm and *ache* on the left one.

We only saw him twice, but I rejoiced in the small details in which we were there. He smiled like you, most of his facial features reminded me deeply of you. I knew you so well by then that it only took a glance for me to recognize us.

The hands were all mine, though. The movements and the disguised clumsiness. He also loved you so much, which was my doing. I could see that even behind the salesman approach.

"That shirt looks amazing on you," he said to you the first time. "You could also just match it with anything you want. You could wear it with jeans or shorts over the summer. You could use high heels, or sneakers, or Adidas. It doesn't matter." He stopped and stared at me staring at you two, "It doesn't matter because, that shirt? That shirt is everything."

He winked. He knew. And we also knew. You bought that shirt, and it does look amazing with jeans or shorts, with heels or sneakers. And it looks so much better knowing our future and our heartaches and the promise of finding us over and over again.

It can become exhausting, though. Not the dying all the time, but the knowing. The thing about knowing is that it makes you question everything. You asked me once, not now, but some time ago, if this was dying or growing up and, to be honest, I don't think I have the answer just yet. It might be both. It should be both. The only difference is that we have learned how to notice them. Both of them. All of them.

THE MAN INSIDE GODZILLA

First attempt

"This is what I wanted to be when I grow up," he said, pointing at a paper scrap that I realized—on a second glance—was an article titled *The man inside Godzilla.*

"I want to write that," I responded immediately, and it was true. I didn't want to write the article, but the sentence. "I wanted to be the man inside Godzilla." It felt like the kind of trait one strives to find in a character. A particular thing that is interesting enough but not too far out. Something tangible and recognizable.

I looked back at him and, because now I knew what was in it, recalled the photo he had sent a few months ago—the one of himself as a kid, wearing a grey sweatshirt and looking straight at the camera. I recalled the small and smart eyes, the curly hair. The cheeks. At the time, it had seemed to me as a cute little performance. A way for him to say that this is what he was, what he is, or a way to push and remember something lost. Now, however, all I could think of was the man inside Godzilla.

"Why?" He was staring back at me, staring at him, in the precise moment of remembrance and nostalgia for the face he used to have as a toddler, trying to discover the physical and emotional traces of that desire.

"I just think it's a good trait for a character. Something that really defines who they are." And this, again, was the truth.

"Well then, write it," he responded. Simple as that.

"Well, then," I smirked back at him. "I will."

So I guess he now requires an explanation. Right? I mean, how do we even build a character when we build a character? What do books in writing theory say about that? Are there even such books? I figured that one way could be to describe how his voice sounded, but I don't know if that is a successful effort to begin with. If I say he was soft-spoken but vehement, passionate—which is a synonym—would that mean anything at all? Maybe if someone else was writing the story, they would say we both were. Vehement or passionate, as synonyms. Soft-spoken.

It was different, though. I used to joke that he was living through the law of making the least effort possible. Not engaging with fights, or opinions, or argumentation. Not engaging in general. Being soft-spoken was just a side effect of his genes and effortless existence. But then again, how important is it for a story to get a definition of the speaker? Is it even necessary?

This is where it could matter, though—the moment when I start to talk about myself. Isn't every kind of writing just an effort in doing so? But anyway, there's a connection here to explore. See, when I was a kid, I wanted to be an equilibrist, but my balance is terrible, and I'm everything but graceful.

I think that, had I said that on the spot of our conversation, this story could be different: The story of how the man inside Godzilla and the equilibrist with no balance fell in love. It is pretty obvious by now that this story is about love, but it could've been so different had I said something else.

Luckily, nobody could know if I didn't.

This is fiction, after all.

Second attempt

"This is what I wanted to be when I grow up," he said, pointing at an article titled *The man inside Godzilla*.

"Really?" I looked at him, making a loud noise while slurping noodles. He had pulled out his phone to show me, and I tried to rush the spoonful. I read a few lines before thinking the sound of the sentence was pretty and interesting. Mysterious. "When I was a kid, I wanted to be a doctor," I replied, cleaning the corner of my mouth with a paper napkin. "I used to think I could change the world, and being a doctor, a medical doctor, felt like the one way to make it fairer. It almost seemed like my only chance."

"Well then, do that. Change the world," he responded. Simple as that.

"Well, then," I smirked back at him. "I will."

At this point in time, though, he already knew what had happened. He knew about how my grandfather had sat me down to have a talk about changing the world and how that doesn't really work. My grandfather knew about making money, and about my hope to become a doctor and move to a place with no doctors. I wasn't even thirteen when this conversation happened. And he said something about how helping others is great, but you either help others, or you help yourself.

"Do you think writers can change the world?" I had asked him that question before. I had even asked that question at the same spot we were sitting this time. The answers had varied, but in general, we both agreed that a writer shouldn't aspire to change the world because, in any case, if people write is to escape something. I am tempted to add some of the specific answers that had been said between us the many times a variation of this conversation had happened. But, to be quite honest, it feels weird to write them in this story. It feels almost like cheating because whatever I say, whichever answer I write down as one of his, will then define who he is and what he believes in. That is what writing a character does to them. While trying to make them complex and interesting, they end up being defined by the smallest of things.

I guess that's why his sentence, his desire to be the man inside Godzilla, caught my ear. The smallest of things.

A detail to define it all.

"The question here is, though," he said, slowly playing with the rice that was still on his plate, "can Godzilla change the world?"

"I don't think that's a question for us now."

"Isn't it?"

"No. You just have to look at the scientific evidence on that."

He laughed.

"Of course," he said. "Of course, a non-medical doctor would want us to look at the scientific evidence."

Third attempt

"This is what I wanted to be when I grow up," he said, sending me the link to an article titled *The man inside Godzilla*. Even though I didn't realize until much later—because he texted me right in the middle of a hectic day, while I was going through classes and work and felt so incredibly tired—by the moment I got home and clicked on the link, it seemed like every single human emotion had vanished from my body.

"That doesn't seem like the best job in the world," I answered, annoyed, adding a bunch of angry emojis.

It wasn't his fault, but when having a bad day, it's always better to blame someone else for the terrible mood than dealing with it yourself. I'm a master of evasion, and having him around, at least through my phone, meant that there was someone else I could always blame. I think he might have done the same, but I can't say for sure. For the effects of this story, we'll say he did, just because it seems like the fair thing to do.

"I hate the subway," he answered forty-five minutes later, "everyone in here coughs without covering their faces. People are so nasty. I just really hate everyone."

"You're so annoying sometimes," I fired back and meant it, my head buried in the pile of essays to grade.

Would you want someone to text you that after a full day of dealing with people? It was so insensitive. He could be so insensitive sometimes. Which is to say, I need him to be insensitive because I want to write a scene in which two characters get into a fight, and it's always very hard for me to do so since I tend to avoid fighting and being angry, and so let things slip away. But if writing is acting, and if you as a reader are performing with me, what better worse trait for someone to have than being annoying to allow me, the narrator, to be petty and angry? What better scenario than a bad day? What worse context than papers to grade without any further explanation?

"Why are you even with me then, if I am so annoying?" My phone lit up with an answer.

"I can't even answer that question without a beer on me," I typed. Then erased. "I have no idea," I retyped. Then erased. I got a sense of fulfillment, knowing he could see the three moving dots, letting him know I was typing. I imagined his frustration bubbling up, staring at the dots as if they meant something. I was, obviously, only projecting.

I finally decided on the most hurtful thing I could think of.

"You are just a placeholder."

Send.

"I didn't even ask you what you wanted to be as a kid."

Send.

"Honestly, nobody cares about coughing in the subway."

Send.

"I don't even like Godzilla."

Send.

I stared at the screen, waiting for the answer.

I knew what I had done, and now I was just waiting for the reaction. Waiting for the three dots signaling he had read me and knew how I felt. I waited for a couple of minutes, putting my phone down and scrambling angrily at a student and their terrible transitions. Then I looked back at the screen. Nothing.

I graded another paper, and then the next one, and still, nothing. I turned on the sound on my phone to be sure I knew when he answered. Not because I was going to look at it immediately, obviously, I just needed to know.

Let's say I stopped grading at two in the morning, which meant it was four a.m. down there. I had not gotten any response. I opened the conversation and typed again.

"When I was a kid, I wanted to be the pink power ranger."

Send.

SWAMP MILKWEED

My first storm did not stop for nine years. I was six, but I still remember the beginning. It goes like this: when the rain started falling, our grandmother marked the date on the pale pink notebook in which she kept a record of all my firsts. With her shaky calligraphy, she stamped the page as *My first ever thunderstorm*. I did not jump at the sound of thunder. My older sister did. Our grandmother, the attentive eye overseeing all things, winked with the half-smirk she gave me when she caught me sneaking out past my bedtime. Every single day after that first thunderstruck, I kept fearing I'd forget the deafening sound of my first storm or the gesture that meant we both, our grandmother and I, knew I was the brave one. It was out of the fear of forgetting that I trained to numb myself to the sound of water and, once lost on it, to recall how bright and how loud it had been.

I was six, so I didn't know the word premonition, but, had I known it, that's what I would have called my first ever thunder—a premonition.

I loved the rain and what it brought: moisture, greenness, mud. What nobody seemed to love was how we lost the comfort and control of our everyday lives. Our calendars and phone books were lost to dampness. The relatively new skates I had been gifted for my sixth birthday, made entirely out of metal, laid rusting outside on our front stairs. Our best dresses remained in their drawers, forbidden to be worn until further notice. The days when our father would bring strange gifts, like mangoes or earrings, were over. I was just learning the days of the week, but when each and every day started to resemble one another, and without reliable measuring devices, I started not to care anymore. Nobody scolded me because it happened to everyone. For a while—it must have been the first few weeks—everyone around me seemed to care less and less about context and measures and courtesy.

There were many theories. Even now, I still hear one or another, depending on the company. My favorite was the one we discussed every couple of weeks during what we called dinner, when our mother was still trying to bring some sense of normalcy by sitting us at the table. With trembling voices, my sister and I would ask her if the sun was dying. By some strange sense of entitlement, we knew that our mother—who is only a vague memory of my childhood—was someone we could trust. She would always answer that it might very well be dead, despite all forecasts saying that it would have to exist for at least a few million years more. "Then again," she would add, serving us a little bit more potatoes or oatmeal, "it's also entirely possible that all of us are already dead, too."

We lived in what I learned many years later was called a highland. That is, we were lucky all the rivers and water beds were far enough and the houses were built tall, as if someone had foreseen the persistent rain. Because of that, the damages to property out of flooding were minimal for almost everyone who stayed. There were other issues: leaks and mold, water stains on everything, our walls alive with lichen. There were also the immaterial damages: all the school days we missed, grades and grading lost to some mysterious archive, everyone who left, crops and pets gone. But nothing flooded forever, and, for a very long time, the only things that were ever constantly soaked were ourselves and our mothers—long-haired and pale—when we wandered outside.

Even now, people ask me if it's true what they say about the rain. I always give the same answer and shrug: at the time, nobody could foresee any danger in it. The first few times I was asked, though, I would add how beautiful it was to live underwater. How great a lullaby the constant tapping of water drops on the ceiling was. How, despite it starting with a bang, my first ever thunderstorm, it tamed and became just a whisper that I would listen to, quietly, as if it was a storyteller. I was six years old, you see. My father was busy leaving, and my mother was busy wandering, so nobody had time for bedtime stories. But I had to learn what people wanted to know. For example how, when it didn't stop for three months, newscasters came over and some of us became celebrities for our melodramatic representation of pain and loss. Or how, when it didn't stop for a year, politicians came armed with trucks filled with black rubber boots and yellow rubber raincoats that smelled of chemicals and plastic. That smell became what I relate with the word *behave*. "It was always the same," I say when asked. Someone came, someone spoke, maybe we got one present or some knickknack that broke and twisted as soon as they were gone, and then we were left to ourselves and our rain for a while again. Sometimes I venture by adding how nobody, not scientists nor politicians or UFO specialists, gave us an answer as to why it didn't stop. But my story, like every novelty, soon turns boring. And the act of telling the story of my hometown, after a while, was reduced to the description of the yearly routine when someone showed up to commemorate the anniversary of the rain and was bored, rather than surprised when, yes, it was still raining.

There are many other stories about the rain that are still my secret. Like how my sister and I memorized fast mostly because, with no electricity and no dryness, we had nothing else to do. At seven, I could recite the first fifty pages of the Pocket Oxford Dictionary. My sister, at eleven, knew all the formulas on the old algebra textbook that had once belonged to one of our ancestors. It didn't matter that neither of us knew what to do with our knowledge. I didn't know what *Oxford University* was. She wasn't sure about how to make sense of all those Xs and Ys. But since we were constrained to the inside world of warmth of our house, our inner world was inhabited with the wild possibilities of a dry future, or any future at all. I looked up the word *university* and memorized its definition, imagining myself living in such a place where words would mean something beyond what they seemed to say on the pages. My sister started drawing her own formulas that didn't really mean anything, except that for her, they did. And slowly, she began to answer the questions on the book, wondering, she told me, if someday she would figure out if the answers were correct.

We also killed time by creating new games using what we had. Our bodies became playgrounds: how many eyelashes can you count? How many freckles have disappeared today? How many new black little hairs has grandma grown in her chin? The windows in our home were our portal: we projected possibilities for what the shapes of raindrops could mean. We created a system to read our fate from splatters of water. News of the world outside the storm did not come easy to us, but imagination did. And in our own secret society of witchcraft, we foretold futures for each other speaking out loud every single possibility we could imagine from our living room.

When I had to say goodbye to my first best friend from the window of the living room shaking my hand—a wrinkly little thing with protruding lines resembling more twigs than fingers—and our grandmother wrote it down so I wouldn't forget, *My first heartbreak*, my sister predicted a great love and a beautiful companionship from a tall, dark gentleman in my future. The memory of the moment comes in flashing images: the bright white cowgirl boots of my friend hopping fast into a car, the face of my sister when she spoke about a never-ending true love, the soles of the boots covered in a mix of mud and wet weeds, similar to the mix we had made before— a million lifetimes ago—to make pretend cakes, the shaky hand of our grandmother choosing a page, the sound of a door closing forever.

It was the white of those boots that I remembered the first time I was on a plane, sitting alone by the window of the cheapest flight I could find. I marveled at the clouds, their constant softness against the clearest blue, and recalled the whiteness of leather against her pale skin. During take-off, I held tight to the plastic armrests on both sides of my body and tried to remember the name of my first heartbreak. I felt my ears popping and, for a period of time, everything happening seemed too unreal. I muttered Laura, Linda, Leo. None of the clouds looked like the clouds I had grown up seeing day after day. Each name came with the metallic taste of mistakes and forgetfulness. The white quality of these sponge-like things seemed to defy what I had until then understood as the sky. I closed my eyes and imagined the sound of falling water to conjure sleep.

Both of our parents went missing. Before the rain, it was mostly our father who left, for days on end. When he returned, he smelled sweet and musky, like fruits that have just started to rot. He would bring small things after these journeys for us, and both my sister and I would jump to his arms at his return. It was out of happiness but it was also out of fear. We would cling our bodies to his as a way to anchor him to our lives. It was a way of letting him know that we would weigh him down into our arms and into our harbor before letting him escape again. A pantomime that meant that we would rather drown him than setting him free. We would chatter loudly and fight for his attention. During the rain, however, it was our mother who constantly disappeared. Sometimes she would grab a tote bag, say she was going to the store, and return a week later. Barefooted. Soaked. Feverish. Other times she would say nothing at all. At her return, her eyes were as empty as they had been when she was leaving. We never greeted her when she returned. There was no anchor waiting for her. Rather, there was a secret shame that the women of the house shared. We looked at her with judgment and defeat. As we stared, our grandmother would prepare a hot bath and demand us to be quiet. At those times, my sister and I would read, comb our hair, and practice new braids, imagining a future in which neither of us looked like our mother because our mother brought no gifts, no smiles, no smells. I was ten the last time I saw her.

This is how I remember that day: our father asleep on the couch, our grandmother helping her pack, and her kissing my sister and me on the tops of our heads, putting on a washed-out raincoat, and leaving. Up in the air, at seventeen, I remembered our mother's voice for the first time in years. Her velvety soft lisp. The way she often seemed to not understand what we were saying. How easily startled she was. How sometimes I would pinch her arms, as a toddler, to get her to look at me. I knew even then I was hurting her, but I remember having this drowning need to feel like she was feeling me touching her.

For many years I wished, to no avail, that in my recollection of that day, she would leave crying. Shedding at least one tear to something she was losing. But every single time I thought about her, the image was the same. Her face coming close, me basking on the smell of her chest, the smacking sound of her lips on my scalp, and my hand running through the spot where she had kissed me, ashamed, trying to erase her trace from my body. There were no tears falling through my mother's face and unto my forehead as a form of baptism. Not one word. As always, my mother bore no farewell gifts. We never spoke about it, but when my sister and I played with our dolls after that day, the mother would always cry. Wail. Beg. As I heard the sound of the door creaking to a close, I looked through the window and heard the weight of her body make splashing sounds until she was completely out of sight. Our mother had left for days and weeks since it had started raining, but this was the first time ever she had taken a raincoat and packed a bag. I stayed still, listening to the sound of her feet squelching over the mud until I lost track of it.

For many years after, I wished I had cried too, but I didn't. Rather, I fell asleep on the floor under the window frame and woke up many hours later, to our grandmother asking me to go wash myself for dinner. Ever since the storm started, I hadn't had a single dream I could remember. That afternoon, however, I dreamt I was making mud cakes from the mix of water and dirt left in the holes of my mother's footprints.

I was glad, for a brief moment on that plane, that the rain made it so hard for her to leave during those first few years. Then, as we were landing and I felt my jaw clenching, I started feeling guilty about that strange joy.

I used to think I had learned everything I knew from strangers. For many years I had no respect for any of the grown-ups in our home—none for our mother, our father, or our grandmother. When I grew tired of chores and of my sister, I would go and hide under the bed in my parents' bedroom. When our mother was there, she would pretend not to notice me and continue to brush her long dark hair. I had a pile of old magazines stacked under the bed. Until this moment, I'm still not sure I ever got around reading one whole article. For the first few years of my life, I understood words only as blurs over a textured page. It had been our grandmother who taught me how to read. With water-based markers, she would draw the letters on the cold white tile floor of the kitchen and make me repeat after her. During the first week of my lessons, I learned how to spell my sister's name, letter by letter, and would spell it out to her, believing I was cursing her. At six and a half, I still couldn't grasp the difference between putting a spell on someone and spelling someone's name. But by seven, with fifty pages of a dictionary on my mind, I had turned into a compulsive and esoteric reader. I had a ritual. At first, I would only pick magazines that were, for some reason, laying around the house. I would choose three or four every month and stare at the pictures: photographs of places wildly dry or lusciously green, people who looked like us, and people who were strikingly different. Most importantly, instruments that seemed as intricate and complex as those mentioned in history books: nail polish, hair dye, teeth whiteners.

The second part of the ritual involved writing stories with what I had learned from those strangers that had been so kind as to explain to me the world through their writing. Unlike the people in our home, these writers had beautiful and complex lives. They knew how to use languages. Many of them, I imagined, had gone to *university*. The first story I ever wrote was about my father. He was a pirate that left us on an island where the sun shone forever. There was no night and no rain, and when he returned, the father brought with him a plastic bag filled with similar artifacts: candy bars, sparkly bracelets, miniature tea sets. I couldn't get enough of reading, and I could definitely not get enough of imagining. Turning pages of a too damp history book, I would start wondering if, for example, like people in places where nuclear explosions had happened, we would also mutate because of our environment. From every birth during those years, I kept expecting—hoping, really—for gills, scales, mermaids. I was sure that I could materialize those things into real life. And if I couldn't, the rain most likely could. Some babies were indeed born with some abnormalities, but no baby was nurtured in the humid air enough to reinvent the way they would inhale their oxygen.

Neither of the women in my family had ever cut their hair. Our grandmother's head was crowned by a long and thick braid that she twisted at the top. Her hair was composed of every shade possible between black and white. When she washed it, the process of drying it in the ever-present rain required several days of us blowing at it with makeshift fans and warming it up with lanterns. Sometimes, my sister would let her hair hang untied and free. Like our mother, she had a dark heavy curtain of slick black hair, and in those rare days where her hair was down, I could see how much they resembled each other. Sometimes, in those days of untamedeness, I would ask my sister to sit in front of me and say nothing. I urged myself to memorize the way her clear brown eyes captured the light, the way her top lip trembled and trapped sweat, and how that reminded me of something our mother did, but I could not name.

My sister learned most of what she knew from our grandmother. She would follow her around for hours on end, cleaning and lurking on every little corner our house had. Despite the rain, after the first year, all the children were requested to return to school. And we did. But she was older, and the little school in town only taught through grade eight. That's why, at thirteen, she decided to stop going. She never made an announcement, and she woke up and went to bed at the same time as everybody else. But after making breakfast, she would return to the bedrooms and start making beds and picking up clothes under the careful eye of our grandmother. "Her dry hands were great for needlepoint," our grandmother would answer when I asked her why my sister could skip school, while mine, always slightly damp and pruney, would stab finger after finger when trying to thread the needle. I missed her at school.

After some time, she started resembling our mother more and more. The dark circles under her eyes turned hollower. She moved gracefully through the kitchen and the living room. Our house had never been cleaner. Our grandmother stared at her, pleased. Our father seemed to be in a good mood as he hadn't been since our mother started leaving. But at night, I could hear a whisper, "when two binomials differ only by the sign between their terms (one a plus, the other a minus), we call this a difference of two squares," or, "a perfect square trinomial results in binomial squares."

I never stopped being slightly scared of flying. Even now, when I look out of the window up in the air, I wonder if it's possible that physics works in the same way that miracles do.

I've never returned home. Never. Every year I secretly tune the local news to see what's happening, how they're celebrating. I see new faces. I see the distorted but familiar newness of the children of people I knew. I honestly don't know what I'm expecting. To see ghosts, I guess— our father, our grandmother, my sister whispering mathematical notions she doesn't really understand.

It was the rain that haunted me. When I catch a trace of lush darkness that follows the deciding steps of a woman about my own age, I feel suddenly cold and shivery. I'm waiting for my second thunderstorm. I brought the notebook with me—its pink cover faded and always seemingly damp. It stops shortly after the first heartbreak, but our grandmother wrote other things in there. Prayers. Spells.

Sometimes I think I see our mother walking around. She still looks the same because memories never age. I see her barefooted and wild, looking at the same time lost and pleased. I see her hands in servers, ads, lovers.

I always saw our mother in my sister, in her industrious warm hands, in the ways she whispered instead of speaking, in the element lost in her eyes. I never saw myself in her. I was also never able to imagine what she would look like dry. But in the end, it was me who took after her. It was me who left life underwater and who never returned. I started dreaming again after I moved to places where the rain doesn't whisper stories to children, and I often have that same dream. The texture of mud on my hands, the almost translucent skin of a body with no direct exposure to sunlight.

When I left, eleven years after that first thunderstorm that soaked everything I knew, it wasn't because I was looking for a dry space to keep growing. I had learned to see life behind a constant veil of water, and it was hard to imagine that, in other latitudes, everything could be as compellingly dry as the photos of deserts and gardens I had seen in magazines. No. I didn't leave because our mother had left, my sister had gotten married, and our grandmother had died. It wasn't because our father was still trying to defend the small barn behind our house from the mold that threatened to ruin the fermentation process of whatever it was he was drinking.

I left because I was bored.

LOUDER THAN BOMBS

For Dario Robleto

It's easy to know. You just have to see them. Not even stare, but see them. In crowds, they'll often turn their gaze towards you. There will be some things they'll know, even without being aware of it. They'll try to protect their questions and wishes. Their pain. They'll see you the way they see wild animals in zoos, almost certain that they're safe. Always just almost. As you greet them, they'll turn somewhere else to find solace. Eyes wild, slipping away like sun-kissed summery children.

Sometimes you'll wish it was easier. There will be days when it will be so loud, so full and dense that you'll wish you could share it. You'll try to guess if there are others. On bus rides, you'll inspect the faces of the commuters and test them. You'll think of all the things you've done wrong and wait. You'll find signs on raised eyebrows and headaches. You'll follow the path of those getting off on corners in which white cars are parked, whisper towards those wearing headphones with music so loud you can feel the rhythm on your chest. Those are the days you will laugh hard enough to feel your body and name it. You'll repeat meaningless words like *transversus abdominis* and *quadratus lumborum* to drain it out. You'll sleep alone with the television on to hear something else—voices, canned laughter. You'll imagine what the people laughing on those tapes dreamed about, what would they sound like. You'll wonder if they're all dead. It will be hard to sleep.

There will be other days. You'll luxuriate on silence, and yet, while it's gone, a part of you will miss it. You'll play music and hum to feel the resonance on your skull. You'll think of your own body as an amplifier. You'll do some research on how amplifiers work and stay inside for days on end—five or maybe even seven, but never ten. You'll be afraid of losing it. You'll wonder what it is. You'll think only of connection and noise. When you finally leave your house, your throat will be dry, and your muscles tense. You'll ask for a coffee, go to the supermarket, take a walk. It will hit you on the face of the cashier or on some girl running around the aisles. Familiar and heavy, like a dream you're sure you've had.

Sometimes it will be useful. You won't be able to explain why or how, but you'll know when to approach someone. You'll know the right way to shape your shoulders as a place for confession. You'll be quiet and listen. People will think your silence is a quality. People will repeat clichés about how you know the right thing to say. You'll answer something about body language and smile like it's nothing. It will resonate inside your skull. When you try to explain it, you'll only think of waves crashing or planes landing. Something between beauty and nausea. You'll wish it was nothing.

It won't happen often, but it will happen if you're lucky: there will be a few days where it's loudest. And there will be things you'll know, then. You'll see someone. If they see you, it will expand like secrets or earthquakes, the knowing. You'll try to hide it, mask the effect on your body. When you get goosebumps, you'll say you're just cold. When they ask if they can sit next to you, you'll say yes with a deep voice even you're unfamiliar with. Your body will feel foreign and occupied. You'll think of the word *territory* and the word *conquest*. The sound will be just as you expected from them. Invisible, vibrating, and soothing. Loud. Loudest. A question mark.

There will be words unspoken, not only fear or wishes. If it works, you'll understand how desire and danger can work similarly. You'll spend dinner trying to locate the source of the sounds. A part of you will know. A part of you will wonder how to describe it. When they speak, it'll stop. You'll discover the pattern happening in the quietness of pauses.

The intensity will shake you. More than usual, who they are will crawl inside your skin and resonate. It will be hard to pinpoint, but, when looked at, you'll feel something boiling underneath the skin. You'll try to understand, and you'll ask them, staring. "What?" You'll say, "what is it?" And you'll mean to ask about primordial things, not only thoughts but mostly fears and wants. You'll laugh about how silly it sounds to imagine things without words only possible between you. You'll feel like breaking a rule when asking. When you do, they will draw a half-smile and say it's nothing. You'll wonder if there's anything real between you. You'll wish it was nothing. When you ask again, they'll look up to the night sky and point to Jupiter. It will make sense that the answer is this planet, however far away it might be. They'll say Jupiter is the most visible in who knows how long. You'll think of luck and coincidences, trying to let go of the necd for certainty. You'll fail. You'll think of all the words you want to share, and immediately after, you'll be washed away by the idea that language is not enough to contest loudness. You'll think, in those exact terms, you love the way they pollute your peace. You'll talk about hearts when thinking of love and noise. You'll talk about rhythm and pulse when meaning to say something about sharing space and time. When they look at you, you'll think of words you've never thought of before to describe eyes: shock, spark, vacuum. You'll tell them how beautiful and machinic language is, and you'll mean how unfit it feels to be uncertain next to them.

They'll see you like a wild animal, too, but they won't feel safe. That power will scare you. They won't hide. They'll wear their pain like they wear their skin. It will be hard to use their noise to help them. You'll stare. You'll try to explain it again. You'll speak of body language and say it's not magic. For the first time, you won't be so sure that's true. "Why do we ask why?" will be a question asked. "Why are you so loud?" You'll whisper when you're close to their body. They won't ask you what you mean. They'll know. When they do it again, give in to the current of their thoughts—electric and loud—you'll both laugh. You'll create touch through sound. When they stand next to you, your arms brushing, you'll hear it and think of feelings. Something abstract. You have never spoken about it, and you won't speak about it ever again, but you do tell them because it's too much. You'll use an ocean metaphor about something wandering in your brain. You'll call it sound. You'll wish you could touch them because you're not sure your bodies can be contained within the limits of skin.

When it's over, and it will be over sooner than you'll expect, you'll say goodbye on door frames or airport security checkpoints. You'll hold on to some notion of loss. They won't ask for an explanation. You won't offer more than your head in the angle between neck and shoulders.

When they leave, you'll try to find similar stories in others. In public spaces, you'll try to catch glimpses of that loudness disguised as nervousness. You'll stare with a hunger you didn't know. You'll crave their pain and desires.

You'll never be a safe place again. You'll hunt for it, like a lion that escapes its cage and bites into someone's limbs. You'll hold the gaze of others. You'll expand or compress your body to be closer to theirs. You'll go to coffee shops or bars and sit for hours, waiting for a prey or a lover. You'll think of them as synonyms. When it becomes too much for you, you'll head back home to take a shower. You'll turn the heat up. Under the falling water, you'll try to remember details: the shape of their fingers, their accent, something boiling underneath your skin. You'll only remember their sounds. You'll go to bed with the lights on. You'll play one song on repeat indefinitely. You'll think of abstract things to make them real. Feelings. Noise. The ocean crashing inside your skull. Humming. Electricity. Touch. Fear. The image of eyes into eyes. You'll sing to yourself what was left unspoken.

If you remain lucky, every once in a while, you'll feel it again: buzzing and loud. It will never be as it was the first time. Nobody could be as lucky. When it leaves you, the sound, the connection, you'll feel slightly emptier. As your body quiets down, you'll try to find Jupiter in the night sky, just to make sure it still exists.

You'll fail.

FLASHBACK

It must have been 1997.

I started first grade in 1997, although I turned six only after the school year started. That is why they wanted me to wait a whole year and come back the next. They let me in, however, because I knew how to read, write, add, and all those things that kids are expected to know when they're starting elementary school. But this is not about my first year in elementary school as a five-year-old. This is a story about me having a younger sister, and about this one photo of us from that time. We look really cute.

She's wearing her hair in pigtails, her leg braces, and her denim overalls. I know she is wearing her leg braces underneath because our mom used to buy overalls for her to hide the fact that she was wearing those braces so that people wouldn't tease her because of that metal and plastic thing holding her together. Talk about body acceptance in the 90s.

We never watched a lot of television, especially not around the time that photo was taken. I remember begging my mom to lie to my classmates of 1997 and tell them that I did watch the *novelas* like they did, just because it felt like that was the right thing to be doing with your afternoons. But I didn't, and neither did my sister. A couple of years later, however, on the weekends we would make sandwiches we deemed as sad because we were both picky eaters. We stayed together, inside the house, sitting on the one huge bed we had created by putting our two singles together, and watched what seemed like marathons of shows that described lifestyles completely different from ours: Cartoons and series with blond-haired, blue-eyed mean girls who wore sparkling short skirts and platform sandals, and who teased Ginger, Lizzie, or Sabrina, as if that was the thing to do to those other girls who did not look like us at all either.

But we still sang along in a made-up language. I think I can almost recall the soundtrack, the tone of the voice. What was it that someone once told her? Something about the grass being much greener?

I don't know if my sister ever got teased because of those braces. I don't think she did, but then again, I don't think I ever asked. More importantly, even if I had asked her, I don't think she would've told me.

I guess she was in kindergarten. She must have been around three. I'm wearing my first uniform, which is how I know I was in first grade, and this was 1997: a plaid jumper, a white shirt, and a burgundy—and incredibly itchy—sweater. I wore a hat for my first day of elementary school because I have always loved hats—they make me feel happy, pretty, and hidden. They did so even when I was five. I know I wore it because there is a photo of me wearing this bright pink hat. But that's not the photo I'm talking about now. In the photo I am talking about, we're standing in the living room of the apartment where we lived for a few years, the one we loved so much and the one we got kicked out of—like the rest of the tenants—because they remodeled it and doubled the rent. But that wouldn't happen for a couple more years and, in that photo, unlike now, we don't know that yet.

The detail is really small, and it would take someone to really look for it to notice, but I don't have to look for it anymore. For me, it's right there: it's the first thing that comes to mind when I imagine that photo. And, to be quite honest, I find myself thinking about that photo more often than I care to admit. When I was a teenager, and we lived in the house that connected both of our bedrooms—my sister's and mine—through a door, I glued that photo to my wall. That was the house where the ceiling of my room collapsed over me, but again, that's a different story, and I don't think I have any pictures of that to remember and celebrate.

Sometimes I wonder what could've happened if... What could've happened if we never had to move out of those first apartments? What if we never had to move? I wonder what it feels like to have a place to come back to, that you know so well you can trace it back in your sleep. If I have to be honest, I don't think I remember the architecture of every space we inhabited in our childhood. I remember the carpets and the ceiling and the cubes of concrete and the skylights, but I can't be sure if any of those things actually looked like I remember them. I don't think my sister remembers either. When we talk about it, about the rooms we shared when we were kids, it almost feels like we are talking about different houses. Maybe we are.

But I remember her. My baby sister. Her I can trace in my sleep. Even now living far away, across borders and oceans, and when her face has changed, I can recall it and say, those are her eyes, that is her hair, these are the many ways in which she is brave, and I'm not.

The apartment building, the one from 1997, had a very heavy glass sliding door. This is something I'm sure is real because I remember the sound it made. Now, if we want to talk about grounding, there are few things in the world so grounding as the sounds our bodies make. I once listened to the sound of a bus running over a kid, and still, to this day, can remember it better than my first kiss because there has never been any other sound like that. Not ever. This makes sense with the story even though it might not sound like it now.

The story I am trying to tell is about my sister, her body, and the apartment where we lived in 1997, but my sister won't really get much say in it.

Maybe that's a better start for this whole thing.

I know for sure I remember this: her small boney hand being trapped while closing the door.

That's it.

The first time must have been an accident. There's no way she could've been plotting for this before that. Three-year-old children come up with lots of weird ideas, but this one required a catalyst. I guess that the first time she was too slow, or the door was too heavy, or a combination of both. What happened was that her fingers got stuck between the door frame and the actual door, making a weird creaking noise. I can still remember the sound of it. It wasn't crashing as much as it was a pushing—something giving in, but only through bending. It's hard to describe the sound a bone makes when it refuses to break, but I felt the vibrations on my chest. Flat and screechy.

The sounds our bodies make help us make sense of the world and our memories, making them more real. I think we all have some of those in our memories. Sounds that are more important than vision. Sounds that are the whole of the memory. My mom freaked out, and off we went to the emergency room. She was fine, my sister. She was too small for her bones to actually break, although it could have happened. Instead of snapping, they bent, so the sound we heard wasn't that of bones breaking. There would be a very long time in my life between this moment and the moment when I actually heard a bone breaking for real.

My sister was three, but she was really smart. She still is. And I guess this is the moment when I talk about how adults speak about kids as if kids don't exist when they are sitting right there. Especially adults who have titles as Doctors or Mothers. She was three, sitting at the doctor's office, and she heard she didn't break her fingers, that they didn't snap, that they only got bent. And this is important, someone was saying that she—my mom, not my sister—was lucky, because taking care of three or four broken fingers on a kid that young can get very complicated. She got a splint for her tiny fingers. They don't make actual splints that size, so the doctor improvised with a wooden tongue depressor and some gauze—enough stability to immobilize a three-year-old with leg braces and pigtails and overalls.

She's wearing the splint it in the photo.

Our mother loved to take pictures of us. We have cardboard boxes filled with artificial memories of things that, for all we know, could have happened in another lifetime to different people. She never liked us looking at them, though. The thing with actual printed photographs is that they can get very messy if you touch them with dirty fingers, which is the state fingers tend to be in, especially when you're a kid. When I moved out of the house, I sneaked a few of those shots—things that wouldn't be missed because nobody ever looked at them. I have a shrine for the polaroid of my mom and me when I was just a newborn. It's a good reminder of a beginning.

I also took that one, the one I am talking about here. Another beginning, I guess—the one for my sister.

When my sister stole money, the one time she stole enough for my mother to notice, she was six or seven. My mother promised she would burn the palms of her hands on the top of the stove because that's what thieves get. She then dropped her off at her ballet class. My sister never shed a tear in front of my mother, but I kept begging her, long after my sister was out of the car, not to do that. It was such a terrible punishment. That's not what mothers do, not how they treat their daughters. It could lead to my sister being taken away, I thought. My mother shocked me when she said, "Stop crying. I won't do anything to her. I just want her to be afraid." I was panicking, but not my sister. And I'm sure that my mom knew that's exactly what was happening. My mom still tells this story about how I kept crying and begging her not to hurt my sister. She tells lots of stories, which I don't love and my sister hates because she was always the troubled child. I don't like them because I think they make me sound like a good child. They make me boring. But I guess I like to hear them because I still learn about my sister's experience in life. When my mother tells a story about our childhood, there are no traces of our father in her memory. I marvel at the erasure of a whole figure, at my mom's ability to vanish him completely. I don't know about the rest of the mothers in the world, but mine, she is definitely a magician.

My sister's fingers were already slightly crooked by the time we got kicked out of the house in the photo and had moved into the new apartment, the one that was trying to resemble a gated community with a park in the middle but where the apartments were so small, we could always hear our parents fighting from the top of the trees we climbed back then. At three, though, she couldn't climb any trees. At three, she could barely stand without falling down, so my sister's favorite thing to do was to buy candy bars and Hershey's kisses from the concession store at our dance studio. She always had a sixth sense for where to find coins in old forgotten purses, on the floor, in the couches. She amazed me when she would dig in her pockets and always materialize a coin out of them. She would hide candy in her pillowcases, inside our shoes, in the metal frame of her bed. At three, she knew that what she was doing was shameful, but she was already developing a taste for that.

The first time, as I said, was definitely an accident. The second one wasn't. It couldn't have been. She was really smart, and even as a toddler, she wasn't the kind of person to make the same mistake twice. I was already in first grade, elementary school, wearing hats and uniforms, but after the second and third times, I started admiring something in her that would only come to have a name many, many years afterward. My sister had a resilience in her that was shocking, pure, and destructive at its best.

"I want to see what it feels like," she said more times than I can recall. At three. At seven. At twelve. At twenty-one. Afterward. Always.

We shared a room in pretty much every house we lived in. We only had separate spaces for a couple of years and when I stayed with our father and she went with our mother. Because of that, we would talk a lot. We always did. Every night, before going to bed, we would turn the TV off, quiet Lizzie McGuire and the adventures we would never be able to live, in the houses we would never see, and in clothes we would never get to wear, just to speak. When we lived in the duplex, with the pretty skylight in the studio but the incredibly dark separate bedrooms, we would sleep together more nights than the ones we spent apart. We talked about death and fears, and we would always sleep holding hands and pressing our cold feet together.

Her fingers were skinny and twiggy, and my hands were always much larger than hers.

She grew up taller than me. Stronger. Funnier. There is a photo of the three of us, my mother holding her the day of her Christening. I must have been two or three. She was a few months old, and my mom was a couple of years older than I am now. There's no way of telling that we would be who we are now by looking at that photo. There is also no way to say that we weren't there, that what we are now is not already bubbling in those bodies in the image. I think I can recognize myself there. I think my mom can too. But I don't really know about my sister, because even though I can see her in the baby squinting in the arms of our mother, when is it that we really start being who we are?

I stopped counting how many houses we lived in after the tenth. I remember them by specific things: the carpets, the windows, the skylights, the ceiling collapsing on me. My mom loved to take photos of us, but she stopped doing it inside the houses, which now I think she did to pretend we had a certain normality to our living situations. I mark the periods of my life, defining them by the houses we lived in. The apartment building in which my sister tried to break her fingers; the apartment pretending to be fancier than it was where we heard our mother scream at our father that she was tired of him not wanting to sleep with her; the duplex where my sister came in running in the middle of the night—blood coming out of her nose—asking if she could sleep next to me; the one with the patio in the middle which we never learned how to sweep just right to please our mom; the big house with my father and how cold it was without my sister; the small apartment where I would constantly ask her to put headphones on while watching TV because I never picked up the habit and did not really care about Grey and her anatomy; all the ones in between, all the ones I can't remember.

Our mother learned how to do the splints

herself. We went to the emergency room too many times, so she got tired of paying, waiting, and always getting just a tongue depressor, tape, and gauze. I started counting but also lost that count after the first ten times. We would try to always keep an eye on her and never let her close to the sliding glass door. But she was thin and small and quick. She was also resourceful and stubborn, and she wanted to see what broken fingers felt like. She was still the same baby who had pushed my mother to close her own business after having her because she would not stop crying; only now, her goal was that experience, the pain. Our parents would try to explain it to her, how it would hurt, how it wasn't fun. They had the doctor tell her, us, what breaking bones entailed. She didn't care. He showed us pictures of exposed fractures. The fracture wasn't a beautiful image, but it was a snapshot of something I understood: the red meat and the fat surrounding what should be kept inside.

IN OUR BEDROOM

You ask me what I'm thinking about, and I can't tell you I'm thinking about bodies. About how they smell. How I like the way bodies form their own scent when unclean, like soil and dirt and the faint rot of sweat and blood, all mixed together with pollution, cigarette smoke, and fabric softener. I can't say this because I don't love you yet and because I know you don't love me either. If you did, if you loved me right now and right here, I would. I would clear my throat and say something like how I like the way the smell of bodies lingers after sex. Or how there is a certain flowery scent on saliva over skin that I also enjoy. I say nothing, nothing really, and turn to face you. I don't want to kiss you, but I do, and when I do, I like it. I feel the warmth of your tongue. Explore the shape of your mouth. You close your eyes when you're kissed, which makes sense. I don't know where it was that I heard or read that you shouldn't trust someone who kisses with eyes open, but since that moment, I do it. Kiss with eyes open. I collect the faces of my lovers in close-ups, all monstrous and senseless. A face is not a face anymore when you stare at it from that angle: the eyes enlarged, the nose a wall. Those are my favorite memories of love.

I bite your ears. Taste your neck and make a mental note of remembering the adjectives salty and long. With three fingers, I follow the path of your hair and pull. Feel your legs barely touching mine, then grasping. After a while, I feel like it's only fair that I get closer. I want to feel your hands on my body, understand the rough patches on your palms, number your calluses. I hope that if I do, the voice that keeps whispering to get out will stop. I roll around, get halfway up, and place my legs around your waist. As I do, I feel my head pulsing, growing into a nightmare. I know the feeling, and I know where it's born. From the window behind your bed, I can catch the glimmering reflection of the bottle back on the table. I had never had whiskey before, and I can still taste it, rich and almost sweet, on the top of my tongue. I wish I felt guilty about this. I try. As a kid, I could feel guilt on command, and it was an easy and blissful state. I still believed then that guilt could only lead to repentance. I wonder—as I run my fingers through your arms—if I will ever tell you this. If we will ever speak of childhood and memories. Then, on top of you, in charge of the view and your face in this light, I decide that I will make a story for you. Even if you tell me the real one. Even if I never see you again. I will create a story for you.

You open your mouth. I know the look of pleasure. Close it again. So close to ecstasy or sanctity. And I want to kiss you whole. Know your skin by heart through taste. But my head is making the room spin, slowly at first, and faster as I push my weight into you. And I wonder if it's possible to sink into someone until they swallow you whole and you're gone forever. But happily. If I could choose, that would be my happy ending. I decide this is something you have to know, so I breathe and move my tongue inside my mouth, if only as a measure to deal with the dryness of it. And finally, after pushing again, I say that this could be a happy ending. You open your eyes first, then your mouth. I can see it behind your eyes: the intention, the looking for the right words, the fear that I might have misunderstood what this is. You don't want to say it, but I know this is only because of how things ended.

I wait for as long as possible and then laugh and get off of you.

There is a space that becomes only visible in bodies together, somewhere between arms and chest and neck, so I make way there. Inhale. The room is covered in golden light, thick and bright. The same color of things I had only known in stories: whiskey or honey or your eyes. You place your other arm on top of me, and it makes me feel so small and vulnerable that I want to laugh.

And even though I still don't love you, and even when I'm not sure I ever will, I still speak. I like the smell of bodies, I whisper, but it doesn't matter. I feel the cadence of your breathing unto my right ear. Sing me to sleep, I guess, I mutter in your bed, alone. My body alive within whatever you're dreaming of.

***

I open my eyes to nothing, only the constant hum of a speaker on without any music coming out of it. No thunder. No rain. I get up, taste metal in my mouth, dryness. Everything seems sharp-edged. The light seems too bright and beautiful to be bearable. I still hear the same voice in my head. Get out. Get out. Get out. The fear of being discovered activates this inside of me, but now I feel almost childish. It's over. The only thing that could go wrong is that you find me searching through your home. I find my way—stumbling—to a confusing hallway. The first time I ever slept on a bed other than mine I was sixteen, and I woke up confused and scared. It was also the first time I ever heard the siren wailing. On the camp set up inside a school gym I stared at the ceiling after waking up in the middle of what seemed such a never-ending night as this one.

I turn left and find an unlocked door. Open it. Turn on the light with a switch, hoping that you have a different kind of light bulb in this room. The light is bright and white—a walk-in closet filled to the brim with photo albums. I decide to stay here for a while.

My mother was strict—no sleepovers ever. She and I followed a routine that laid out the energy of my everyday life until we couldn't. When we had to leave our home that first night, to gather at the gym turned into a shelter, she asked me to put her wedding ring in my mouth and say nothing. She covered her earrings with cotton balls and placed them inside a pill container.

"Nobody is going to raid our home," I wanted to say to her. But I wasn't so sure, so I put the ring under my tongue and stayed silent. My memory of that night, the very first night of our war, is tainted with the taste of metal. I did not speak a word that night. We never returned home.

On the third album, I find it. I wasn't looking for anything. How could I? I had never been to your home before. But still, there it is. The lucky one. A small picture of two children among pictures of family gatherings, births, and what seems like parties. In the photo, there are two toddlers, and it's hard to tell, at that age, if they are boys or girls. One has its back turned to the camera, so I don't know what they look like. But the other one is facing front, so I stare at their curly hair, eyes closed, a gesture of pain. They are embracing. The one whose face we can see has their arms around the neck of the other one. The one whose back is on camera has their arms around the other's waist. In the background, a white-walled home, a well-kept garden, the rest of us, unaware. It looks just like what I imagine a photograph on the edge of the end of the world would look like.

Hopeless and beautiful and innocent.

I haven't seen a photo album in many years, probably since I was a toddler myself, so I don't remember exactly how to set one up, but I decide to keep this picture. Carefully, I lift the corner of the translucent sticky paper, put my hand on the cardboard, and pull the photo. The operation is quick and silent. I go back to your bedroom feeling dizzy and intoxicated.

For the very first time since the sirens wailed all those years ago, I also feel relieved.

***

What does this mean? I had a friend who would ask me that question over and over. What does this mean if, for example, the world does end, he would say. Or, what does this mean if they set a curfew, and we never see how we look in the moonlight? It was not a question but a strategy. A rhetorical question—she would reply if someone complained—is not meant to be answered but reflected upon. And even back then, I wanted to have the right answer. I wanted to be the one who said that it mattered because we mattered. Because we existed and were bodies, and we could love. I never said anything of sorts because I was too scared to have the words come out of my mouth and then being unable to stop speaking. I thought of words, then, like a current. Something inside the digestive system rather than the brain that once flowing would never stop.

I was a quiet child.

I met you in the streets last night. Or was it tonight? Both of us starry-eyed and confused and not happy but so, so close. I knew you had seen me slouching through the rubble. I knew I had seen you seeing me. The story could end there, but I went over and asked. What does this mean? I did not ask you anything about the war or about fear because that was not what I wanted to know about you. And you stared, fully understanding why I asked you. Then, you opened your mouth and kissed me with eyes closed. That was the right answer. That was the only possible answer.

***

You're still asleep when I get back to your room, and something breaks inside me. I'm overwhelmed with thoughts and images. Let's not wake up or start a new life. Let's not be afraid. Let's just talk until we know everything about each other, and there's nothing else we can possibly say. And when I say everything, I mean everything. When were you born and what was your favorite color, or how you discovered fear. Let's not eat or move away from this room. I want to drink another of your whiskey bottles. The whole thing. I want you to kiss me with the taste lingering in my mouth. I want to observe your face when you do: all pale skin and freckles and lines. I want to trace your body, the silhouette that contains you, with the tip of my fingers. I want to dig my nails unto you. I finally realize this is what it feels to not be at war: bodies together, pleasure, whiskey, and something. Not love, but still something.

But again, I say nothing. I kneel next to my backpack—containing everything I own—and try to quietly put the photograph of the two kids inside. Then I get on the bed next to you. Sitting. I examine the room and try not to pay attention to the drunkenness or the hangover, whichever is happening at this point in time. Still, I feel my arms heavy and my neck stiff. I wonder where you keep the water and realize I don't know if this is your home, if you grew up in here, playing and hiding through the long hallways. Or if you, like me, have walked confused, clinging to the walls for protection. During the first year, many people fled, leaving their houses empty. It was only a matter of time for people like us to start squatting. I had found most of my favorite things in places like these: small rocks, necklace pendants, real chopsticks. All useless and beautiful. It makes me feel slightly happy to imagine that all these things are not yours. Like both of us are pillaging someone else's life. Maybe I could be the wife, and you could be the husband, or the other way around. That would explain why we know so little about each other.

***

For many years I had the same nightmare. My mother and I are leaving our home in the midst of confusion and darkness. Most of our neighbors are doing the same, walking hurriedly with a look of fear in their eyes. Kids are crying though mothers ask them to be very still and very quiet. My throat is dry and my mouth watery because I'm scared of swallowing. I have my mother's wedding ring underneath my tongue. All of those images recreate almost exactly the scene from when we left our home. Some of the neighbor's faces are blurry or changed, and I can't exactly remember how my neighborhood used to look like back then, so the scenery is sometimes completely different. Other times I see the streets and home clearly, but they are laid out as they were the last time I saw them— houses destroyed, holes on the ground.

Then, as we're about to get to the shelter, I do it. I feel the muscles of my throat, the tension of my esophagus. And I know. I have just swallowed everything we had connecting us to history and pride and our home. I don't say anything, but my mother stops immediately and turns to see me. As she does, she looks less and less like my mother. She starts growing, her hair, her arms, her head. Everything gets bigger until I can't see her fully, and I try to follow her eyes because I'm sure that she'll forgive me if she looks me in the eye. She'll know that it was a mistake and that I'm sorry, tired, and scared. But she never looks at me. Or I can never find her eyes, as she gets so very tall and endless. The only thing I know is that I can't really breathe anymore, and I know it's because the ring is inside me. My throat or lungs or somewhere closes off because of it. In real life, I still have the ring. I also have her earrings and the pill container she hid them in. Turns out nobody wanted jewelry. The dream, however, always ends the same way. My mother, or the creature she has turned into, declares that she has to have the ring, that she'll have to extract the ring. I always wake up before the extraction.

***

You ask me if I believe in god. Any kind of god. We've been in this house long enough to have heard three records until we memorize them. You have a great memory, better than mine. At some point, you also start dancing. There is no real concept of time, and it doesn't even matter. The war is over, anyway. I tell you I don't really like dancing and I don't believe in any god. You say that you find it strange. I want to ask you why, but I know that's exactly what you want me to do. I know you want to preach something about believing or faith that I don't want to listen. Instead, I finally ask you if the house is yours. You answer quickly, as if you were actually expecting this question, and the fact that I finally ask it relieves you.

"I live here," you say.

"So, what does that mean?"

You wink at me, and I want to kiss you now. Again.

You smell of dust and salt. After you take a shower—this house still has running water, a mystery we celebrate by taking long showers—the space between your collarbones and shoulders turns into a different color. It's shiny and aqueous. Translucent. That's my favorite part of your body.

I know now that you were 20 when the war started. I have told you I was barely 16. I still don't know everything about you, but sometimes, I call you love. As mothers would call their babies, convinced I know now what the word means. You don't like it when I call it *The War*, but that's the only word I have for it. Let's find you a dictionary, you say. We're both orphans. But not only because we've lost our parents. Everything about us is orphaned. There is no hometown, no city.

We shouldn't have happy memories, but we do. I still don't tell you about my favorite things: the photograph I stole from this house, the way mouths taste after drinking, the smell of bodies, your long fingers covering my eyes when you play that one song.

"What do you call it?" I ask you one morning.

"The what?" you reply.

"The war."

"It was never a war," you respond somber, sitting up. "There was never a war. There was only fear, control, and those things that make people spiral out of control and leave, or do the most horrible things."

"So, what do you call it?" I insist.

"I call it *The Sentence*," you say. Before I ask you why, you continue, "because someone decided it was happening, someone placed the punishment on some other, and we happened to be standing in the way."

LOVESTORY

1.

It came to me late at night. I was asleep, and then I wasn't. Suddenly it came out of my mouth, and that was that. I didn't notice because it was late and dark, and I was, as I said, half-asleep. But the next morning, there was a strange taste in my mouth. Something earthy and foreign. There also was a change in the air. The apartment felt stuffed. Rarified. You know the feeling of being observed you get at airports, malls, or the subway? It was like that, except that I couldn't pinpoint why. In those places—airports, malls, and subways—you are actually being observed. I guess I was too, but at first, at least first thing in the morning, I couldn't notice. There was no way for me to see it. It would take more space, and it would become visible, just not then. Not at that exact moment.

2.

I guess it is my fault. Not that I extended an invitation, but it was me who called for it. Calling something, naming it, is a sort of invocation—a name, a spell crafted for christening.

So yeah, guilty.

3.

It's hard to define what a name really is. Even now, I still don't think I can. These are the facts I know: we all have one. We all use one. We fixate on the sounds and the shapes of the letters that compose it.

But what is, actually, a name? Is it part of you? Do you receive it or gain it or grow into it? Don't get me wrong. I don't have answers. It was only that, up until the moment it started living with me, I had never before given it a thought.

What is your name, for example?

What if I mispronounce it?

Is it still your name?

4.

I found it because I almost stepped on it. And after being found, it grew, kind of how a voice would. Wavy, if you know what I mean. It was tiny and soft at the beginning. It's hard to define how it is that it had a texture or a color, but it did. Sticky and velvety and pastel are good adjectives. Or they used to be, when it was tiny. Squishy and shiny. One could even define it as childish. But then it started occupying more space: growing angles in abrupt places, softness and roundness where one would expect edges. Sometimes it would be at the table in the dining room and shift color. Other times we would find a new finger or ear while taking a bath. Once, it grew some hair while sleeping on my side of the bed. It was interesting and amusing. It was also unexpected. And, to be frank, it could be quite messy at times. But I was a gracious host because, you see, I named the name, so it was my issue to deal with.

5.

I don't know either what you love when you love. If you love a skirt, do you love the skirt as an object, or do you love the way it looks on your body? In which case, do you love the skirt or do you really just love you? I think the same applies to any kind of love. Not that it's good or bad, but how could we know what is it that we love when we claim we love someone? And, if we grow into our names, if we claim them as a part of us, a part of us someone can love when they love all of us, how could I not love it? It was mine, after all. I had summoned it in my sleep. I had fed it, and nurtured it, and swept the hairs it shed, and clipped its nails, and gave it permission to use my computer and eat my apples when I wasn't home. So if that's love—and it has to be—how could I not love it?

6.

It spoke slowly, softly, only ever learning to be self-referential. Just one set of sounds coming out of it. It had different tones though, so we could communicate. Or we imagined a way to do so. We created our own tonal language for our everyday routines. So I can say surely it not only existed, but it loved particular things: bad music from the 80s, bananas, shiny rings. It also hated particular things: Taylor Swift, tomatoes, big stones. But what my name loved the most was being read to and being caressed in one particular spot that became harder and harder to find as it grew.

7.

I grew fond of the routine: leaving in the morning for work, coming back in the afternoon, calling from my office a couple of times throughout the day. But while I think I found it slightly comforting to know that it would be there by the time I came back, that I wouldn't have to be alone if it was raining, cold, or snowing, it was painful to know that it just couldn't leave our home. How it never went out. And, as it grew, it needed me more. Or I needed it more. Or, maybe, we created a need for each other.

I started calling in sick to the office. A couple of times over the first few months. And then a couple of times over one month. And then a couple of times over a week. I should've known better, but it felt so good to be needed. After a while, it happened. I called it *The Miracle*. It was the morning I looked at it, and it had a sort of light blue halo exuding from its skin as it slept. I couldn't bring myself to leave the bed. Even breathing felt difficult when away from it. I wondered what would happen if I just stopped everything. Working. Speaking. Leaving. All of it. I would just turn the TV on and play another episode. (By then, we had already figured we loved particular TV shows, especially badly made, cheaply produced reality shows. Nothing

like the Kardashians. More like *Toddlers and Tiaras*).
I would just turn my cell phone off and unplug
the wifi. And since imagining it felt so easy, I just
did it.

That morning, after the haze, I made strawberry
pancakes for breakfast and played Ariana
Grande while we danced in the living room. I
felt, for the first time in my life, like I was where
I needed to be. I was bathed in the realization
that, finally, I would find my own name inside
my own shape-shifting body. And I was so very
happy and dizzy that I called it once, and again,
and again. I named it, and it joined me in the
repetition of the only word it would ever learn.

This time, though, we spoke with purpose.

8.

It might just be a human thing. To hurt what
one loves. A human fault or condition. I have
never met someone who doesn't do it. We all
just fuck up once in a while, and when we do it,
we fuck up particularly the things we care about.
Like love or lovers. Like naming. Like pouring
wine on top of your favorite skirt. So I'm trying
to say that yes, I was guilty of keeping it, and
nourishing it, and making it learn things about
bodies that it probably shouldn't have learned,
because it was still just a tiny name that had to

grow up so fast. But don't say I held it against its will or corrupted it, because I loved it. I really, really did. I didn't care about the world because I loved it. And I don't know how many people can actually say this and mean it.

9.

I never meant to hurt it, but it kept growing bigger and bigger. It took over the master bedroom, so I had to move all my things to the studio. It had already claimed the bathroom, the picture frames, the air. It was always hungry, and we were running out of money. I kept feeding it bananas. Sixteen for breakfast, at least. Sometimes I couldn't find its mouth, so it would go for days without eating. The bananas would rot, and we would get fruit flies. And I just couldn't do that. I just couldn't let it starve. I still think that was love. I remember how I did find it. How some people look forever for it. Sometimes I still dream about it, and when I wake up, I feel it was the best thing ever, or the closest thing to that. I proceeded slowly. I read at it so it wouldn't be scared. Poetry. It bled, which was surprising, but its blood was thicker, and it wasn't red or, at least, not red as we think of the color red. Back then, we were both stripped of meaning—no colors or words between us. We were both hungry bodies, growing and named. Me, after my grandmother. It, after my dreams. We belonged. The last story I told it was the story of the poet who wouldn't name her creations. And then it was gone. I couldn't breathe anymore. There was hair everywhere. I kept on sweeping the house and peeling bananas for hours.

10.

I let them tangle in my throat now. I try not to sleep too much and set alarms every few minutes. I can't remember the last time I dreamed, and I believe that's for the best. I feel them. Crawling and trying and hungry. So many names. So many of them.

PITCH

I want to watch a movie about me. A movie about a girl who sits alone in her house for hours, not talking to anybody. A movie about a girl who goes to 24-hour cafés in her pajamas at two in the morning and flirts with the cashier while she buys two gigantic cookies because she just fucking feels like having cookies. A movie about a girl who crosses an imaginary border every month at least. A movie about a girl who crossed the border to go to an unexpected funeral and cried at the airport. A movie about a girl who has no recollection or link to her past and gets an MFA trying to write a whole thesis about that, running out of ideas so often that, instead of writing, she just clicks on random YouTube videos and learns everything that's happening in the current season of *My 90 days fiancé*. I don't want it to be a drama, though. Erase the part of not talking to anybody. Or, even better, don't erase it. Make it a sort of comic relief.

I want to watch a movie about me. Not about a girl like me, or a girl that looks like me, or a girl that looks like what some Hollywood director thinks a girl like me should look like. Make a note for the casting call to say Mexican or Latina, but remember that the girl should be what her mom calls *yellowy* as a joke, brown with thick straight dark hair and small almond-shaped eyes and a relatively large nose. Think of someone that can be confused by a white European with a girl from the Philippines if she has bangs and long hair and moves to Europe.

That's the type we're looking for.

I want the movie about me to be an Independent Film on a Budget That Wins Awards In Some Foreign Festival™. The more laurels around the name of said festival, the better. Because the movie about me will be a subtle but pungent critique of the state of the system. Every system. Even the system of my shower that keeps breaking every couple of weeks. Include the quote, "I might wear pink lipstick, but I'm still punk as fuck," that can be easily spotted on my Twitter account. It will probably become a feminist film, or what critics will claim to be a feminist film. Maybe even a cult film, who knows?

I want to watch a movie about me that ends with something that leaves the audience with a happy-sad feeling. (Like in *Sing Street*. Like The Cure). I already have the final song picked out, so now please clear the rights for *When I Grow Up* by Fever Ray. Let the final credits roll up while she sings about all the things she'll do when she grows up: become a ghost, a forester, a monster, a pirate. I chose it just for one sentence because I, too, put my soul in what I do.

I've always been quite dramatic. I guess I mention it because it might be relevant to the scene where I'm about to quit college and then find this song and sing along, and it gives me some relief, and I don't quit college, and I get to go to Spain and lose twenty pounds because I can't really afford to live in Spain, so I'm always starving, and then come back and read even more books, and move to another country and regain the weight after all. In that specific order.

Don't make the movie about the body, and don't play the song until the very end, either. It would make no sense with the logic of the narrative, and we all know how important the logic of the narrative is.

In the movie about myself, we need an all-female cast, and my sister has to be beautiful, and Andrea has to be beautiful, and Fernanda has to be beautiful, and Valentina has to be beautiful, and I refuse to show how they are all broken because I'm really tired of movies where beautiful girls who are friends end up fighting or alone or in therapy or married to beautiful boys whose only merit is to look them straight in the eye and state how obviously beautiful the girls are. I refuse to let any of them, or even me, become the manic pixie dream girl, no matter how much I wanted to be one of those as a teenager, although that might be an interesting plot twist.

I refuse to let the audience go, "Oh, I understand her," because they don't. Instead, we'll have their characters not letting themselves cry, sitting at cafés at two in the morning with gigantic cookies in front of them while the Me character stares at them with all the love she is capable of, holding down the tears while it rains. It has to rain for the cliché to work. The audience will never know what's happening behind the window. The camera will shoot this from the outside of said café, clearly. And they will only be able to see the beautiful girls who refuse to cry. *Trátame Suavemente* in the background because Gustavo Cerati can't be a love interest, but he has to be present in the movie somehow. *Trátame Suavemente* and the rain that falls.

The conversations will remain our secret.

So, I'll tell you what I want: in the movie about me, the movie that I want, that I really, really want to watch about me, there will be girls eating and crying and texting each other at midnight to ask, "am I more Ravenclaw or Hufflepuff?" There will also be girls getting wasted and dancing to cumbias playing in the background, mostly Selena, holding hands on a dance floor, refusing to dance with guys, and laughing at them. There will be a lot of traveling and reading and concerts and days where everything gets really quiet.

Painfully quiet.

In the movie about me, I will have my Bowie phase, and I will do cardio listening to *Space Oddity*. I will also have my Caifanes phase and will sit for the long hours of my commute whispering the lyrics to *Mátenme porque me muero*, and I will start a campaign—or a hashtag really—to #MakePlaceboGreatAgain. And I will love all the girls in the cast. And I will replay the scenes with them in my head as flashbacks, a meta-movie that takes place in memory. And I will write them love letters when I can't get up from my bed after Donald Trump gets elected. And the audience won't go, "Oh, I get her."

The audience will cry.

Ugly cry.

Like Kim Kardashian Ugly Cry.

And the movie about me will be one of those movies that people don't want to see because they are too scared of the power of their own sadness, but will see anyway because someone tells them it will be worth it. Like *The Grave of the Fireflies*. And some of them, some girls, but mostly guys will say, "this movie is too fucking long." And they'll be right. It has to be too fucking long. But others, mostly girls, but also some guys, will say, "This is the movie about me that I can't seem to find on Netflix. This is the movie I've wanted to watch all the times I've ended up watching and rewatching *The Breakfast Club*."

Acknowledgments

This book could only be possible in community. None of the words here could have ever been written if I didn't have the support and the love of the people who have stood and believed in me—even at times when I can't—and in the power of imagination and language. While none of the stories here are exactly autobiographical, each of them is somehow rooted in real love, real relationships, and real heartbreak. It's that reality that allowed fiction to permeate imagination, and it's those relationships that supported me through the process of trying to carve something beautiful out of pain and memories. Some of the people are already named in the stories, but I need to take space here and honor the love of everyone involved in this writing process. Because, again, this book exists because they exist and, luckily, we crossed paths.

Thanks to Zachary Bushnell and Valentina Calvache for creating a haven of love and dancing when California tried to swallow us whole, for the shared secrets and universes, and for making me forever one-third of a trinity.

Thanks to Darío Zárate for the world of beauty we created together, and the memories of that love which will forever nurture this world. To Dario Robleto for finding me in a moment of deep self-doubt and sharing with me what intensity can mean, especially while the weight of the world was too heavy. To Migueltzinta Solís for remaining, after years and distance, a reader, a friend, and a cheerleader who dares me to keep writing. Thanks to everyone who helps me stay grounded when I feel like it's impossible.

To my Houston family: Criseida Santos—the best roommate—who shared so many beers, nights, and advice with me. Saúl Hernández, who has become a brother through our migration processes. Jesús Cruz-Garza, a true friend, found in the most unexpected of places. José Peña, for all the gossip. And Eric Todd for many challenging conversations.

To my Mexico City family: María Fernanda González, who is and will forever be my anchor and best friend. Daniela Rea, whose hugs erase the pain and heaviness. And Nayeli García, who is such a bright light that shines through our shared darkness.

To all the friends in many geographies, thanks for remaining an eternal source of inspiration, strength, and trust. To Emi and Naira for making up stories with me. To every friend in Guadalajara who has been my home at times: Grisel Pajarito, Tlacaélel Camarena, Carlos Gallo, Angel Olvera, Fernando Azul, Alejandra Carrillo, Mariana Recamier, Emmanuel García. To Valentina Jager—a friend through time and space—for adopting this introvert, dancing with her, and taking the time to create the most beautiful and perfect cover a first-born book could ever ask for.

I wish I could also thank here all the songs, movies, books, and conversations that shaped me and this book; but that would be a list so long and incomplete that I just want to thank the fact that music, literature, art, and friends to share them all with, exist.

I had the chance to work with the best editor for this book, and I'm forever thankful for his patience and dedication, and for believing that these lullabies were good enough to exist in the world. So, thank you, Alejandro Rodríguez, for reaching, reading, and working with a chaotic person like me. Willing a book into existence and working for it to exist are two very different journeys, and I'm happy we shared this one with each other.

I also want to thank all the editors I've had before: Kasia Juno from *Carte Blanche Magazine* and her dedication to making my Lovestory the best story of love it could be. And Kitty Galloway and Sydney Bollinger at *Camas Magazine* for giving Dark Matter a positive space to be alive.

I also want to thank David Izazaga and Héctor Farina for believing in me more than a decade ago and never abandoning that belief. To Dr. Rivera Garza, without whom none of this could be possible in the first place, thanks for giving my second language a home in writing. And to Yuri Herrera, for being the first reader who, in the shortest of notices, agreed to devote time and attention to these stories.

Finally, I want to thank the four most important people in my life. While this book has been around six years in the making, it has taken a lifetime of being allowed to create and imagine to get here, and none of it could've happened if I hadn't been raised by humans who believed that quiet girls who bring books to birthday parties deserve to try, fail, and keep trying to find themselves. Thanks to my mom and dad for allowing me to grow up in a way that always had room for more stories, for allowing me space to find myself in unexpected decisions, for letting me travel far and wide, and always having room in their homes and arms for me at my return. Thanks especially to my mom for holding me through all the pain and challenges that writing brought and will—hopefully—continue to bring. Thanks to my little sister, who remains forever my greatest source of wonder and inspiration, and without whom I wouldn't exist as a complete person. There's nobody in the world who better understands me than you, July, and I love you with everything I have. You might find yourself in some of these stories, and I hope that if you do, you'll smile with memories of who you were through my eyes. And to John, my heart, forever my best reader and provider of books, thanks for pushing me to keep trying and to not give up, and for believing I have something to say. I hope this book gives you the thrill I've experienced every time I've read your words. But if it doesn't, you know what? You are the beauty in my next.

BAKSTENEN HUIS PUBLISHING B.V., NEDERLAND

CPSIA information can be obtained
at www.ICGtesting.com
Printed in the USA
LVHW020257160321
681607LV00009B/324